JEAN'S BLACK DIAMOND

Jean's
BLACK
DIAMOND

A Story of Australia

by Deborah Bennett

Illustrations by L. F. Lupton

CHRISTIAN LITERATURE CRUSADE
Fort Washington, Pennsylvania 19034

CHRISTIAN LITERATURE CRUSADE

CANADA
1440 Mackay Street, Montreal, Quebec

GREAT BRITAIN
The Dean, Alresford, Hampshire

AUSTRALIA
P.O. Box 91, Pennant Hills, N.S.W. 2120

NEW ZEALAND
Box 1688, Auckland, C.1

SCRIPTURE UNION in NORTH AMERICA
U.S.A.: 38 Garrett Road, Upper Darby, Pa. 19082
CANADA: 3 Rowanwood Avenue, Toronto 5, Ont.

SBN 87508-684-5

PUBLISHERS' NOTE

Deborah Elizabeth Bennett, then a schoolgirl aged fifteen, submitted her story, " Jean's Black Diamond ", for the C.S.S.M. Literature Competition in 1947. The judges awarded her the second prize, and were impressed with the promise of this young writer. A number of reasons have contributed to the delay in publishing the book, but it is now sent out in the hope that many will enjoy this Australian girl's lively tale of her homeland.

I

"O-O-O-OH!" Jean Brownley reined in her horse and sat gazing with some excitement at the band of brumbies* that were racing down the valley beneath her. Startled by her approach, the stallion had quickly herded his mares, and headed them towards an opening in the rocky walls that surrounded them. As Jean watched the flying figures, she saw a beautiful mare, black except for white socks and a white diamond on her forehead, racing easily past the others and almost catching up with the sorrel stallion. She was built to perfection, and she galloped with ease and grace that left Jean gasping. Presently an uprooted gum, five feet high, loomed up in front of the stallion. He jumped it neatly, and the mare followed, clearing the obstacle as if it hadn't been there. The girl mounted on the high-mettled roan gave another gasp, and suddenly realized she had fallen in love with the black mare at first sight. Her beauty, grace, speed, and power

* "Brumbies"—wild horses

9

held an appeal for Jean that could not easily be forgotten. She remembered what her father had said only two days previously—" I wish we could buy more horses. That poison weed has carried off nearly half the herd." " Those brumbies," Jean thought now, " I· wonder if we could catch them? " She turned Pepper, her gelding, and cantered quickly home.

John Brownley owned a once-prosperous cattle station in the Great Dividing Range, just south of the Queensland border, and he bred horses—at first it was a side line, but it had, by now, developed into his chief interest. Because of a weakness in his boundary fence, much of the stock, cattle and horses, had broken through to eat the poison weed which meant certain death to them. So the family had been compelled to live on a greatly reduced income, and sometimes the children would see a worried frown on their parents' faces, as they discussed the bills that were so hard to meet.

Mr. Brownley and his wife had told their children to pray often and earnestly for success with the stock in the coming spring, and as Jean galloped towards the homestead she realized that this must be an answer to prayer, and her heart sang as she offered her thanksgiving. Dismounting near the stable, she was met by Bob, her seventeen-year-old brother, who instantly demanded the reason for his sister's excitement.

" I've just seen," she explained breathlessly, " a whole herd of brumbies down in the valley, not far from Ghost Cavern—only on the other side of the fence, of course! They were beauties! I saw them galloping towards that western opening—gee! and the stallion was just *it*! Sorrel ; powerful, too, and pretty quick. And, oh! "— and here Jean's face lit up once more with ecstasy—" there was the most beautiful mare—black, with a white splash on her nose—like a diamond—and white socks. And the way she ran, and jumped! " Jean unsaddled Pepper, rubbed him down, and turned him into the horse paddock before following Bob into the house. " It'd be good if we could catch them," the boy said, agreeing with Jean's proposal; "see what Dad thinks."

As the family sat down to tea, Jean told the others of the wild horses. "Don't you think we could catch them, Dad?" Bob asked eagerly. "You said we needed more horses, and Jean says they're pretty good stuff!"

Mr. Brownley, a strong, burly man, thought for a while, and then consented: "Yes, it would be a good idea ; don't you think so, Mother?" In everything the station owner looked to his wife for her opinion, and now the tall, strong-faced woman replied, "I think it's an answer to prayer". "That's just what I thought!" exclaimed Jean excitedly. "Oh, Dad, we'll have to do it tomorrow! I know it'll be worth the trouble." (Here Mrs. Brownley hid a smile, for she well knew how much her daughter loved mustering.) "I saw them jump a huge boulder, and they're magnificent! And there's one mare ..." Pure bliss crept over Jean's face again, but she felt she could not speak of that horse—*her* horse, as she had felt instantly.

So it was arranged that the morrow, which was Saturday, would be reserved for catching the brumbies.

"Can we come, too?" asked Frank, a boy of ten ; and Margaret, two years his senior, echoed his question. But their father's face showed stern refusal. "You're too young to be herding wild horses—you'd possibly get hurt, or play around too much, if I know *my* family at all!" Mrs. Brownley, seeing the two disappointed faces, suggested that the mischievous youngsters could open the gates, and with this consolation the pair waited expectantly for the next day.

Jean found it hard to sleep that night. Many times she sat up and gazed out of the window, on to the moonlit peaks and dark valleys, imagining herself out there among the horses—even riding her—yes, *her* black mare—Black Diamond! Oh, what a name! She would call her 'Black Diamond'!

And suddenly, Jean thought of another thing—would her father let her have the mare? Oh, if only he would!

If only she could tame her, befriend her, ride her. . . .
Jean's heart was pounding in the stillness. She thought of
herself being, perhaps, the only one able to ride Black
Diamond! Things like that had happened, she knew, for
she had seen it here on the range. People had caught
brumbies and tamed them, and sometimes a horse would
attach itself to its owner, who would be the only one able
to manage it. Ever since she could remember, Jean had
been a true horse-lover, and with the love she gave to them
had come a curious, inexplicable power over all animals.

At last, her eyelids drooped, her head nodded, and Jean
fell asleep.

Before dawn next morning, the family was astir, and
preparing for the busy day ahead. After a hurried breakfast, the best horses were saddled, and the party, including
Mr. and Mrs. Brownley, Bob, Jean, and two of the four
station hands, turned their horses' heads towards Freshwater Valley, where the brumbies were most likely to
be.

They rode along in the stillness of morning, and after
trotting for some time Mrs. Brownley discovered a hoof
mark, and then another, and another, until, arriving at a
muddy waterhole, they found the ground covered with
tracks all leading in the same direction. As the waterhole
was close by Freshwater Valley, the imprints were unmis-
takably those made the previous day by the frightened
herd. "They're fairly fresh," Bob remarked, "it's them
all right." The party followed the tracks for nearly two
miles before Jean sighted the herd grazing peacefully on
a small hill some distance away. "Ah!" grunted Mr.
Brownley triumphantly, "now for it!" The riders
separated, to close in on three sides of the hill, leaving the
side nearest the station the only way of escape.

The huge sorrel stallion was standing a little apart from
the rest—head erect, eyes roving, ears twitching, nostrils
quivering, mane and tail flying gaily in the wind. As he
stood there, proud and magnificent, even his captors sat
silently, paying homage to his splendour. And then, a

scent that carried danger reached those quivering nostrils,
Instantly, the nervous body twisted round, and as his eyes
fell on the humans quietly approaching him, the stallion
neighed his urgent alarm, and with amazing speed and
skill he herded his mares. But it was too late. The riders,
so terrifying to the brumbies, closed in upon the herd. Ah,
there was a gap—a way of escape! With a shrill scream
the stallion led the frightened mares and foals southward,
unknowingly heading straight into captivity.

" Where is Black Diamond? " Jean wondered anxiously.
She did not wonder long, for there was the beautiful
creature that had won Jean's heart, galloping easily to the
front of the racing brumbies. " There she is! " Jean
shrieked, " Black Diamond—look at her! " This call
was unnecessary, however, for every eye was watching
with wonder the graceful movements of that lovely
body.

" After them! " shouted Mr. Brownley, and the party
gave chase. " Head them off to the left . . . into the top
paddock! " But the wild horses were not to be caught
like that. The wise old stallion led his band towards the
mountains. " Head them off," Mr. Brownley yelled,
" Quick! To the right! "

" If they go into those gullies, we'll never get them ! "
gasped his wife. But they did not go into the gullies. Pepper,
an excellent stockhorse, caught Jean's urge to hurry, hurry,
and putting all his strength and speed into the work,
managed gradually to overtake the racing herd. Flourish-
ing her stockwhip with skill, Jean shouted herself hoarse,
until the brumbies, terrified at this strange tormentor,
changed their course and veered towards the top paddock
once more. " We'll get them yet! " cheered Bob, who
had caught up to his sister. " Keep them straight on now,
and they'll go for the gate."

"Yes," agreed the girl, " but how are we going to get
them in the gate? They'll possibly turn on their tracks
and stampede! "

" They ought to go in, with six demons yelling at them

from behind," Bob returned optimistically, " here's the gate . . . look ! "

The brumbies were milling excitedly around the gate which Margaret had opened. Shouting and yelling, the riders tried in vain to drive the stallion through. " Some-one get round that side and whip the stallion ! " roared Mr. Brownley. Just then, Margaret and Frank appeared, apparently from nowhere, brandishing two stockwhips, and while the others looked on in amazement, the two galloped up to the rearing stallion, one on each side of him, and by dint of many blows across his back and rump, forced him to go through the gate.

The rest was easy in comparison. The mares readily followed the stallion, and at each gate there were always two people to force him through with whips. At last, after much exhausting work, the brumbies were trapped in a small paddock, where they milled around nervously.

Now their captors had time to inspect their prizes at leisure, and Jean, looking for the black mare, found her rearing frantically in the centre of the herd. " That stallion's a beauty ! " Mr. Brownley enthused, " and those mares are pretty good." He surveyed the yearlings that were running close by their mothers, and added, " A fine crop of colts, too ! "

Black Diamond was more spirited than the other mares : she revolted against this captivity, and distractedly sought a way of escape. There was none. The mare, more finely-tempered than the rest, knew the only thing to do. She knew that this fence, nearly six feet high, was separating her from freedom, and so she must overcome it. Isolating herself from the mob that was surrounding its leader, Black Diamond cantered quickly to the other end of the paddock. Approaching the fence, she gathered herself together, and with one flying leap cleared the obstacle with inches to spare.

Jean gasped, and instantly threw herself into her saddle and was pursuing her horse before the others could recover their breath.

A long-drawn-out whistle escaped Bob's lips. That effortless leap over what they thought would baffle any horse, left all the onlookers dumbfounded. " After her ! " shouted Mr. Brownley, " she'll clear the other fences, too ! " The others sprang into action at his words.

As Jean pursued the mare, she prayed, " O God, do, *do* let me catch her ! " The horse reached the next fence a moment before her pursuer, and jumped it easily. It was a low fence, and Pepper cleared it well. Jean urged him on, and then, swinging her lasso expertly, she brought the mare up with a jerk that nearly threw her on her haunches. Then, to prevent the horse from choking, the girl galloped up to her and slackened the rope.

Mr. Brownley came dashing up to help his daughter, and riding close to her, took the lasso from her as she unwound it, and wound it around his own saddle horn. Black Diamond, terrified by this strange thing around her neck, reared and plunged for several minutes before her captors could coax her back to the paddock. They finally succeeded in bringing her between the two horses, who seemed to give her confidence, for she followed quietly.

Back at the paddock, Mr. Brownley tied Black Diamond to the fence, and as it was now past noon, the family turned toward the kitchen. Jean lingered behind ; she felt she could not leave her horse—there it was again—*her* horse—that persistent thought; from the time when she had first seen her, it had seemed to be *her* horse. For some reason Jean loved Black Diamond more than any other horse she had known, and with that love came a feeling of ownership.

As Jean approached the wild-eyed, angry mare, a thrill went through the girl that she never forgot. She murmured softly and soothingly to the restive horse, and after some time Black Diamond, yielding to that strange power which some people possess over animals, became quieter. Jean stayed for a long time, feasting her eyes on the horses which gradually lost their fear of her, and then, answering a summons from the kitchen, she sped away for dinner.

Seated at the table in the spacious, airy kitchen, Bob couldn't help remarking, " Gee ! I reckon that was pretty all right, you going after that mare ! "—which, coming from Bob, was praise indeed. " Oh," returned his sister, " I couldn't have held her if Dad hadn't come up just then."

" Anyway, I'm proud of you, girlie," Mr. Brownley chimed in; but Jean replied quickly, " Well, I asked God to help me, and He did."

Mr. Brownley finished his chop before saying to Jean, " What did you call her, out there on that hill ? " The girl looked up eagerly, and said, " ' Black Diamond,' Dad. Don't you think it suits her? " " Yes, I guess it does— she certainly is beautiful, too. What speed and power ! And her jumping ! I reckon she'll be worth her weight in gold ! "

There was a pause, and then Jean went on, " Dad, what are we going to do with Diamond? She's too valuable to go with the brood mares." Mr. Brownley considered, looking for help at his wife. " I think we could train her for a hunter, or even a high-jumper. She'd sell for a good price."

At the word " sell ", Jean's heart missed several beats ; she had not thought of that. " Do we have to sell her, Dad? If we trained her, she'd get good prizes in the show . . ." Her voice trailed off, for Mrs. Brownley had broken in, " Jean, dear, you know how things are now—we badly need the money, and she'd sell for far more than we'd get for prizes in the show."

Jean felt a lump rise in her throat, and looked down at her lap. At first, hot rebellion rose in her cheeks. ' She's my horse—they can't take her away . . .' But Jean was a sensible girl, and after a struggle she told herself, ' I'm being stupid, really, *and* selfish. Here I am, living among all the horses I could want—it isn't as if she was the only one ! '

Bob, who understood his sister almost better than any-one, tried in vain to console her. " Aw, gosh, Jean," he said

gruffly, " you'll have her all the time she's being trained."
This, however, only made Jean worse.

When the meal was over, all the family worked with a
will, and soon the washing-up was completed. " I'll have
to overhaul the cattle before I let them loose," remarked
Mr. Brownley. " I'll want some help in singling them
out. . . ." He looked sideways at his children. This was
the signal for them to jump up and demand to help their
father, for they all loved the hard, vigorous work of the
country. Today, however, although the others showed
their usual glee, Jean responded only half-heartedly. Since
dinner, something seemed to have left her. Bob had not
failed to notice this, and now he tucked his arm in his
sister's, saying softly, " Like to come for a walk, old girl?
Dad won't want us yet." Jean threw him a grateful glance,
and together they left the kitchen for the grassy slopes a
little distance away. " It's no use moping," reproved the
boy, in a brotherly way, " it won't get you anywhere, and
you won't be any happier."

"Oh, Bob," the girl exclaimed, the lump rising in her
throat again. " If only you knew how much I love
Diamond ! "

And here the strong, tough tomboy gave herself up to the
most bitter sobbing. Bob was distressed. " Aw, gee ! " he
comforted, " fancy you lassoing a wild bolting horse in the
morning, and howling away like nothing on earth in the
afternoon ! "

The pair sat down on the grass, and Bob put his
arm tenderly around his sister's shaking shoulders. " I
say, you prayed about catching Diamond, and you
caught her all right, so why don't you pray about
this ? If God sees fit, He'll make it as right as rain in
the end."

Jean lifted her face, and a new light crept over it. " Why,
of course ! " she responded, " I'm being stupid ! Bob, let's
pray about it now ! "

So together they bowed their heads, and out on that
lonely hillside they asked their Heavenly Father to help

and to strengthen them as they faced this problem, and to show them what was best in His sight.

"I feel better already," smiled Jean through her tears. She had fought her battle and won, and with renewed fortitude they hurried to the paddocks to help with the cattle inspection.

2

JEAN awoke with a somewhat bewildered feeling. What was today? Oh yes, Sunday. What had happened yesterday? Why, of course, Black Diamond! At this thought Jean sat up suddenly, and looked out of the nearby window. Something drew her, irresistibly; after committing the affairs of the day into God's hands she read her daily passage from the Bible, and hastily dressed and went out into the fresh, invigorating, early morning air.

The sun had just risen over the mountains amid a glorious curtain of red and gold, and the girl thought to herself, " It's nearly time to milk the cows. I'll go and see Diamond before I bring them in." She ran lightly to the horse paddock where she stayed for a while, admiring the mare, and sometimes speaking softly to her. With a little

sigh Jean went on to a farther paddock to collect the cows
that provided the milk for all the station inhabitants.

At the cowshed she found Bob, Margaret and Frank
busy with the machines. The four always milked the cows
as just another of their many jobs, and the milking-machines
made light work of it. The routine was rather hurried
today, for the little Union church which the Brownleys
attended was many miles away, and thus made necessary
an early start.

Soon after nine, the family and the hands (Dick Harris,
Ron Smith, Clive Richardson, and Max Weston) saddled
their horses and trotted quickly down the mountain side.
Arriving at the church, the family filed in quietly to sit in
their usual pew.

In the sermon that morning, Mr. Marsh, the minister,
explained how futile it is to bear our own burdens, instead
of casting them on to the great Burden-bearer. Bob looked
at his sister and gave her a wink full of meaning, and Jean
smiled back. Bob had his ' burden ', though none except
Jean knew it. For in Bob's heart—ever since he could
remember—there had been a great desire to be a doctor ;
but the boy, practical as he was, had quickly realized that
because of the great loss of stock there would be no means
of giving him the education that he longed for, and he must
therefore put the idea right out of his head. But the old
desire continued to gnaw at his heart, and sometimes Bob
would grieve for the forbidden goal.

After the service some of the congregation (those who
lived far away) gathered on the lawn behind the church
to eat the lunch they had brought with them.

As Bob and Jean munched their sandwiches, a little apart
from the others, the boy remarked, " My word, that was
a message for you ! " His sister looked up. " And for you,
Bob," she replied ; " you know what you told me yesterday,
about praying for Black Diamond? Well, why don't you
pray about your wanting to be a doctor?"

" I do ! " Bob was a little indignant. " You know
I pray about everything."

Jean was silent for a time, and then answered, " Bob, I mean praying *with faith*. You're trying to put this idea out of your head, because you think it's impossible— that it can't be realized ; but with God, nothing is impossible."

Bob looked at his sister for a moment. " I say, you're right ! " he said at last. " And in future, I'll pray about it, believing that God *will* give me the means of training, if it's His will."

After lunch, Mr. and Mrs. Brownley and the hands went into the church for the afternoon service, while the children gathered on the lawn for Sunday School.

After tea, the talk gradually drifted to the horses again, and the family discussed which horses should go with the brood mares, and which should be trained.

" Dad," Jean questioned eagerly, " may I train Black Diamond? "

Mr. Brownley considered. Jean was not yet sixteen, and had her studies to do . . . but the girl had given her love to that mare . . . to train her would be useful practice. . . . He looked at his daughter's pleading eyes, and consented. A grin of joy lit up Jean's face. " Of course, you mustn't let this interfere with your other work." " Oh, no, Dad ! " promised the delighted girl, " and thanks awfully ! " " You can start tomorrow afternoon," her father continued, " I'll give you the entire responsibility of taming her, breaking her in, and training her. You're fairly sensible, and you can do it with care."

Jean's delight knew no bounds. She found it harder than ever to study her correspondence lessons next day. (The boarding-schools had closed down, because of an outbreak of infantile paralysis.) She was not brilliant, though she was clever enough to get through her exams. ' Bob's clever,' she thought, over her history books, ' he's got the brains of the whole family. Poor old Bob ! I wish he had the chance of training for a doctor. He'd be good at it, I know.' But Bob had left boarding-school two years previously, when he was fifteen, and it didn't seem fair that the eldest child should just stay at home, helping on the station.

With difficulty Jean brought her thoughts back to the voyages of Captain Cook, but her mind wandered again. Black Diamond . . . what if they could sell her for a large sum? . . . and the other horses . . . perhaps Bob *could* go to Uni. But to sell Black Diamond—her horse, that she was to train—suppose it meant Bob's happiness? Jean swallowed hard. This was her battle.

The dinner bell rang out, and the girl thankfully put her books away for the day.

After the midday meal, as soon as the last dish was wiped and stacked neatly on the dresser, Jean dashed out to the horse paddock. That morning, with the aid of her father, she had turned Black Diamond into a small adjoining enclosure. " How old do you think she is, Dad? " she had asked as they had shut the gate.

" No more than one-and-a-half," he had replied. " It's a good thing we've got her so young."

As Jean opened the gate into the breaking-in paddock, Black Diamond whistled shrilly, and reared high. The girl stood watching fearlessly, and praying to God to keep her safe and to help her. The mare continued to rear, pawing the air savagely with her forefeet.

Suddenly Jean dug her hands into her jodhpur pockets, and quietly turned round, backing the horse. Very gradually the rearing ceased. Black Diamond, baffled by this strange animal which stood there so calmly, cool and unafraid, stretched her neck forward to sniff curiously toward the girl. Apparently she liked the scent, for although she jumped back a pace the mare leaned forward with less fear to sniff again.

Slowly Jean turned round to face her horse ; Black Diamond reared again, and retreated to the farthest corner of the enclosure. Jean sat down quietly on the middle rail of the fence, and began to read a book produced from her pocket. Once again, the black mare was baffled, puzzled and curious.

After some time, which to Jean seemed like hours, Black Diamond took a step forward—a slow, hesitating step, but yet a step ; and then another, and another. Jean read on, and turned a page, not knowing at all what she had read ; then, raising her eyes, she coaxed in a soothing, low-pitched voice—her 'special' voice, used for calming frightened animals.

Diamond stood stock still, wanting to go nearer to that strangely comforting sound, but lacking the courage. The low current of talk was something she had heard but once before—the previous Saturday—something which soothed, encouraged, and fascinated the nervous mare. Jean talked on for some minutes, and then quietly left the paddock.

Taking a bridle from a post where she had left it, the girl gave a peculiar whistle, and Pepper came trotting up from the shade of a tree. Jean rubbed his nose and neck for a moment, and then, slipping the bridle over his head, she mounted and rode bareback up and down the paddock.

Black Diamond watched all this with puzzled curiosity. This fact was taking shape in her intelligent mind : here was one of her kind who came up to the strange creature fearlessly, who let it touch him, and get on his back. Perhaps this creature didn't want to harm her ; perhaps it wouldn't hurt her.

For the sixth time, Jean drew near the breaking-in paddock, and this time she dismounted and gently un-bridled her steed. Then she opened the gate and led Pepper into the paddock, retreating after having given him a quick rub down.

Left alone, Pepper began to graze, while Black Diamond advanced cautiously towards him, anxious to satisfy her curiosity. Drawing near, she again caught that scent of the creature that walked on its hind legs. It was the scent of humans, and the mare felt that it held something pleasing and nice.

Presently Jean returned with a small bag of oats, which she poured into the feed box, and Pepper at once began to munch the fodder joyfully. Black Diamond was very

hungry: she watched her companion for some time, and
then followed his example, finding the new feed very
acceptable. Thus they were left all that afternoon, the
companionship breaking down some of the black mare's
fear.

In the evening Jean came to the paddock once more, and
completely ignoring Black Diamond (which she found
hard to do) she led Pepper away to the horse paddock,
soon returning with some hay.

These performances were repeated every afternoon for
a week. Black Diamond was kept in the small paddock,
just large enough to allow a certain amount of exercise.
Every day Jean would stand and talk to the mare in that
same soothing, encouraging tone, or else she would ignore
her ; and daily, she would bring Pepper in, taking him
away at night, till Diamond began to look for the girl that
she was learning to trust.

Then, one day, when the blossoms were pushing through
the boughs, and the swallows were returning, and life
seemed full of hope, Jean came to the paddock with one
pocket bulging.

She whistled Pepper, and brought him into the enclosure,
where she held out a lump of sugar. Pepper ate the morsel
with obvious pleasure ; Black Diamond, looking on, wondered what this was, and advanced a little to investigate.
Pepper ate a second piece, and then Jean held one out to
Diamond. The mare jumped and retreated a pace, but
came forward again as the girl gave the piece to Pepper.
Jean extended another lump, coaxing and reassuring, while
Diamond held her ground, eyeing warily the proffered
sugar.

Thus they stood for some time, Jean, with one hand out-
stretched, the other feeding Pepper, who was enjoying the
treat to the full, and Diamond, nervous, excited, curious,
and longing to come near and snatch the titbit from Jean's
hand.

" Come on, girlie, come on, I'm not going to hurt you,"
the patient, encouraging voice crooned on. " Come on,

then, you'll like this, come on, don't be afraid . . ." And then Jean held her breath—her heart was pounding as if against a drum, for the wild, untamed mare was reaching out . . . further . . . further . . . her neck was stretched . . . further, until the quivering lips had snatched their prize. Jean's mouth opened with the pure ecstasy of being the victor over the creature she loved.

Diamond had drawn back hastily ; but now, as Jean offered another lump, the beautiful head reached out again, and with less hesitation the mare seized the delicacy ; finding it to her liking, she stepped forward with more confidence for the third lump. Now the sugar was all gone.

Jean walked away, and coming back after a few minutes she went up to Pepper, rubbing him gently and arranging his mane. Then, leading him out, she mounted and rode around the big paddock without saddle or bridle—a feat which requires much practice. " Good old Pepper ! " she exulted, as she turned him loose, " you helped me a lot, today."

Approaching the house, she saw her father looking over the other brumbies. " Dad ! " she exclaimed excitedly, " I did it ! Black Diamond took three lumps of sugar out of my hand ! "

A twinkle came into Mr. Brownley's eyes as he said, " Well, well ! Fancy wasting sugar on an animal ! " He laughed as he added, " Yes, my dear, I know. I was watching you, and I think you've done very well with that mare."

"Oh, I prayed about it, Dad, and anyway, Pepper helped to encourage her." Jean was always modest. " I think it was a good idea to put him in with her, don't you? "

" Yes," agreed her father, " and now these mares will have to be sorted out. We'll have to break them in first, and then we can pick out the best for training, and the others can go with the brood mares. " We'll have our hands full."

"Gee, Dad, can I help? "

"Yes, I'll need all the help I can get. You can come out in the afternoons, after you've done your lessons."

Around the tea-table later, the family discussed the breaking-in of the brumbies. "We'll start tomorrow," Mr. Brownley declared finally. "Bob, you'd better ride over to the men after tea, and tell them to prepare for some hard work tomorrow—remind them to look over the saddles, and make sure that everything's safe." Bob nodded, and when family prayers had ended, he ran off to deliver his message.

"Let us help, Dad," pleaded Margaret. "I don't know," was the response, "you won't be riding those brumbies, even if you can sit a bucking horse. But maybe there'll be something you can do."

"You four must be very careful," warned Mrs. Brownley, "you don't know where you are with wild horses, and one of these days one of you will be picked up in pieces!" "We're all right," Bob assured her, "we'll promise to be careful, won't we, kids?" The three agreed, and hurried to bed to get the needed rest for the following day.

3

"BR-R-R-R-R ! It's cold ! " Bob jumped out of bed and ran into Jean's bedroom, where the girl was sleeping peacefully. In the midst of her dreams her pillow was taken from under her head, and placed on top of it.

" Wake up, lazybones ! " her big brother teased. " Beloved, it is morn. Arise, shine, and shake off dull sloth ! " Jean mumbled something, and turned over, opening one eye. " Wake up ! " repeated Bob, shaking her gleefully. " Breaking-in today ! "

His sister sat up, wide awake. " Why, so it is ! Fancy me sleeping in ! Well, absent thy person, and I shall clothe me. Begone, I say ! " Bob chuckled, and made his exit.

Once outside, the pair were joined by the small fry, and they all hastened to the horse paddock, watching the mares with interest.

" They're pretty well used to the paddock now," remarked Frank. Presently the children moved on to Black Diamond's paddock. The mare grew uneasy in their presence, so they left her and went to bring in the cows.

Their track led over a number of paddocks, until it climbed up the steep side of a hill (it was too small to be called a mountain) named the Swagman. Half-way up this the cows were grazing peacefully, and at the sight of the children they moved slowly towards the homestead, where a good feed of corn awaited them.

As the sun gained height and warmth, it flooded the landscape with gold, bathing the meadows with light, and tinging the peaks with glory. The beauty of the dawn was never lost to the Brownleys, although they saw it every day. The milking was soon completed, and the four made their way to the kitchen, where the aroma of bacon and eggs drew them as if by a magnet.

" I wish Dad would let us help with the horses ! " Margaret grumbled. " Fancy doing lessons when you know something exciting is going on outside ! "

" You ought to be grateful," Bob reproved. " If you were still at boarding-school you'd be doing lessons all day instead of only in the morning, and you'd miss the breaking-in altogether."

" Bob's lucky," Jean countered, " I wish I were a boy, 'cause then I'd be riding the broncs all day." Jean hated missing anything like this.

" Too bad," sympathized the fortunate Bob, " but anyway, you'll be breaking Diamond in, remember. You'll get your full share of bucking then."

When breakfast was finished Mr. Brownley rose hastily, for there was little time to spare, and said to his elder son, " Come on, Bob, we'll have our work cut out to put those horses through."

As the boy followed his father into the warm sunshine, Jean looked after them longingly, feeling that she would have given almost anything to go with them. After helping to clear away the remains of the meal, she and the youngsters repaired to the wide, shady verandah to do their lessons.

Jean studied hard, hoping to get finished in time to visit the paddocks before dinner. She waded through grammar, French, maths, and history, and thankfully stored her books away for that day. It was only half-past eleven ; there was almost an hour before dinner, so Jean left the house for the scene of the breaking-in.

As she did so, she heard a commotion in the paddock, and saw one of the brumbies, with saddle to one side and reins dangling beneath her head, galloping wildly towards her. Seeing Jean, she changed her direction and fled towards the house.

Mrs. Brownley, also hearing the noise, rushed out, and was instantly confronted by the bolting horse. As she came close Mrs. Brownley grabbed at the reins ; the mare dodged, but she was caught. Mrs. Brownley threw all her weight on the reins, till Jean dashed up to help her, and with their united strength they managed to restore the mare to the paddock.

There they found the men bending over a prostrate figure, whose leg Bob was immobilizing with a sapling and a lasso. Some of the hands were converting two saplings and some shirts into a stretcher, and as the two approached, Mr. Brownley, who was watching Bob's quick actions with silent admiration, said briefly, " Dick Harris. Thrown from that roan mare. Bob thinks his leg is fractured."

" Mother caught the mare ! " grinned Jean. Her father's eyes widened ; he looked over at the tied mare, and then at his wife, and remarked, " Good for you, dear."

When Bob had finished applying the splint, Dick was lifted on to the stretcher, carried to the kitchen, made comfortable on the settee and given a cup of strong, sweet, black tea by Mrs. Brownley.

Bob telephoned Doctor Rex, who promised to come out fully equipped after hearing the nature of the injury.

Around the table at dinner, the family fired questions at each other about the incident. " How did you come to be outside, Jean? " " You haven't lost your technique, Mum ! That was a good catch ! " " That roan mare looked a tough proposition." " How did you fall, Dick? " and so on.

" How are you feeling now, Dick? " questioned Mrs. Brownley.

" Oh, I can take it, missus," was the gruff reply. " It's not so painful since Master Bob fixed it up."

" Yes, Bob, that was pretty good, but how did you know what to do? "

The boy reddened, stole a sideways glance at Jean, and answered his mother with a casual, " Oh, I just read it somewhere in a book."

" You must have studied to purpose," Mr. Brownley put in shrewdly. Bob reddened still more, and stared at his plate, while many thoughts and reawakened desires raced through his mind.

" Well, to the work, to the work ; come along, Bob," and the two men left the womenfolk to clear away the dinner things while Margaret and Frank helped to pass the time away for Dick.

Mr. Brownley and his son arrived to find the efforts of the men more successful now that the disturbing element of the roan mare had been removed. The two had just lassoed more mares, preparatory to saddling them, when Jean came running to the paddock, her chores finished. " Dad," she begged, " could I hold their heads while you saddle them? "

" You're not strong enough," Mr. Brownley answered, but Bob cut in quietly, " You know, Dad, Jean's got a way with animals . . . she might help to quieten them." The father looked from his son to his daughter, and chiding himself for his foolishness, he reluctantly agreed. Jean stepped up to one of the mares and firmly grasped the rope that was swinging from her head. With that soothing, comforting voice, the girl reassured the restive horse, holding her firmly yet gently while the saddle and bridle were put on. Then Bob mounted, and Jean loosed her hold quickly.

The enraged and frightened mare shot up into the air, arching her back like a cat, and landed on stiff forefeet. With a peculiar twitching of the skin near the withers she instinctively loosened the saddle, making it more difficult for Bob to keep his seat. However, he managed it until the fourth jump, after which he sailed gracefully through the air and reached the ground with considerable emphasis. He scrambled to his feet, wiping the seat of his pants.

Meanwhile, Mr. Brownley had saddled another mare, and was putting her through the usual routine. He stayed on for three minutes, and then his wife came into the paddock, clad in grey jodhpurs.

"I've come to help, dear," was the brief explanation, "seeing you're short of Dick's help."

Mr. Brownley surveyed her a little doubtfully. He didn't like to see his wife hazarding—well, perhaps her life—as a buck-jumper, but when the labourers were few there was nothing else to do.

The breaking-in was continued for some time, until most of the mares had been partly reduced to submission. The great sorrel stallion was to be sold to a neighbouring station which wanted a new stallion, and his breaking-in had been the masterpiece of achievement.

Just as Mrs. Brownley was preparing tea, Doctor Rex arrived. He immediately attended to Dick's leg, confirming Bob's diagnosis that it was a fractured tibia, and commending the boy for his prompt and skilful treatment. Bob blushed with pleasure and pride at his words, for he had spent many an hour at night secretly studying first aid, anatomy, and more advanced medical subjects.

Dick's leg was encased in plaster-of-paris, and he was transferred, by means of the crutches the Doctor had brought with him, to the men's quarters. The crutches were to be used for at least six weeks, which did not please Dick.

In the evening Bob and Jean caught their horses and rode over to Mount Guardian, the eastern boundary of their property. Under the brilliant moon the range was painted a delicate silver, and the pair rejoiced in the beauty of God's Creation as they cantered slowly up the mountain side.

"We won't have time to reach the top," said Jean, as their steeds slackened on the ascent, "but I wish we could. I love to see the moonlight on the snow."

They reined in their horses and sat silently surveying the peaks above them and the valleys below.

"We'd better start moving," urged Bob after a moment,

and he turned Ranger, his white gelding, to face the home-stead.

"Bob, look!" cried Jean as she prepared to follow, "there are our horses . . . see? Down in Evergreen Valley." In the moonlight one could pick out the far distant figures of the stallion, brood mares and colts that belonged to the station. Charger, black, powerful, and magnificent, was keeping watch over his band—nearly thirty in number—and he showed some uneasiness at the sight of the riders on the mountain side.

"Come on," said Bob after a while, and the two horses stretched out in a homeward gallop.

*   *   *

While the elder children were admiring the stallion and his herd, Margaret and Frank had gone to bed, and Mr. and Mrs. Brownley were left alone.

"You know, my dear," remarked the man, "I had my eyes opened today." His wife turned an enquiring glance at him.

"When I saw how that boy handled Dick's leg—well, I realized with rather a shock that he knew just what to do, how to do it, what the symptoms were, and all the rest. He seems to have a flair for doctoring."

"Yes, I noticed that ; and the way he acted when I mentioned it at dinner."

There was a pause, and Mrs. Brownley continued, "I have known for a long time that his ambition is to be a doctor . . . look at all those books that fill his bookcase ! Medical journals, and all that ! "

"He never mentions it," her husband interposed.

"Perhaps he realizes that we haven't the means of training him," was the answer, "but yet . . . I wonder? If we could sell those brumbies for a good price—they'll make good hunters, and hunters are in demand now—and still manage on our present income . . ." She broke off, and Mr. Brownley said thoughtfully, "It takes about £2,000 to train for a doctor."

" I know," said his wife, and was silent.

Out in the paddocks, Pepper and Ranger were turned loose, and their owners walked slowly towards the stable to put away the bridles. Inside Bob, something seemed to be bursting: he felt he couldn't contain himself any longer. Since the accident, that day, when the necessary knowledge had come automatically to his mind, the old ambition and longing had welled up within him as never before.

" Oh, gee ! " Bob exclaimed now, with a note of desperation in his voice that Jean did not miss. " Gee ! How I *do* want to be a doctor ! "

Jean responded to that urgent plea by giving all the comfort she could. " Bob, when Black Diamond is trained, she'll bring a large sum—and the other horses, too ; perhaps . . . perhaps then you could do the training ! It may be the answer to our prayers ! "

Bob's look was tender as he replied, " But surely Dad won't sell Diamond—something'll have to stop him ! You love her so much ! "

They linked arms, two comrades in distress. " Oh, I *know* it will come out all right. God will undertake. We must keep on praying hard, very hard ! "

Bob secretly marvelled at her faith . . . his sister shamed him sometimes. " You're a real help, Jean," he said gratefully, " I do try, but I'm afraid I'm pretty weak." His sister squeezed his arm affectionately and replied, " Aren't we all? " It was in moments such as these that the deep understanding between them made itself most evident.

Next morning at breakfast, Mrs. Brownley said, " It's about time to let the cattle out now, isn't it, dear? "

" They should have gone back ages ago," her husband replied; " perhaps Jean and the youngsters could do that this afternoon."

So after dinner the three repaired to the cattle paddocks to drive out the steers to their summer home on the range. It was easy work, for the cattle, anxious to be out in the open spaces, did not need much driving once the gates were opened.

The children escorted them through all the paddocks to the hills, where the cows and steers would spend their spring, moving upwards to the mountains in the summer, returning to the hills in the autumn, and wintering again in the homestead paddocks.

Ruffles, Barnacle (Barney), and Scamp, good cattle dogs, helped the children in their task, and the cattle were soon wandering freely among the hills and dales.

On the return journey, the dogs scented a rabbit and gave chase, finally killing it. " Here, boy," called Margaret, " come on, Barney ! " Barney came, the rabbit in his mouth, but as he approached he spied another rabbit, and in his mad rush to get it he knocked heavily against Margaret, bowling her over so neatly that a roar of laughter went up from the other two. The victim clambered to her feet, covered in dust, and smiled ruefully.

" Any breakages? " joked Frank. " Yes, I've broken my peltsis." Jean was puzzled, for she had little knowledge of the skeletal structure.

" It's my haunt bone, or something," Margaret explained.

A light broke over Jean's face, and she collapsed with laughter. " You mean the pelvis," she giggled, " the haunch bone ! " And to herself, " I'll have to tell Bob that, and see what he thinks ! "

There was some time to spare before tea, and Jean decided to spend it with Black Diamond.

As she opened the gate of the small paddock, she drew from her pocket a carrot, and offered it to the mare. Diamond stood quite still, undecided. This was the girl who had given her that beautiful sweet stuff a few days ago, and here she was again, presenting something else mysterious, so what harm would there be in taking it as she had done the sugar? But Pepper was not there—that horse whose presence gave her courage and assurance. Black Diamond's senses were strained, striving to ascertain that all was well, but the mare was still wild, unused to humans, fences, houses, noise ; she would not venture it.

Finally Jean walked out of the paddock, whistling Pepper, and instantly Diamond wished that she had taken the proffered gift. Pepper trotted up and munched the carrot contentedly. Jean led him into the paddock and left them, returning with more carrots.

" I did it before," she thought determinedly, " and I'll do it now."

She gave a carrot to Pepper, and then offered one to Diamond. The horse hesitated for several minutes ; at last she moved forward. With her free hand Jean fed Pepper with two small carrots, and then Diamond reached out and snatched the titbit. It tasted delicious, and the mare soon looked for another. With growing confidence, she munched the carrots, with Jean talking in a low, even voice. So, step by step, Jean steadily pursued her patient plan.

4

" HEIGH-HO ! " yawned Jean as she awoke early one spring morning. " What's going to happen today? Oh, yes ! Black Diamond to be halter-broken. Oh, boy ! "

She jumped out of bed, stretching luxuriously ; then she spent her regular morning quarter of an hour with her Bible and in prayer, asking for patience and guidance with Black Diamond.

Dressing quickly, Jean hurried out to see the horse, who by now looked for her daily appearance. During the past weeks the black mare had learned to trust the girl completely. She would now let Jean handle her—and in the girl's touch the mare was conscious of nothing but tenderness, love, and understanding. Black Diamond had grown accustomed to hearing her name, and learned to like it.

Jean stepped into the morning sunshine, thinking, ' Why wait till this afternoon to break her in? I'll do it now ! '—and ran to the stable to get a halter. Then, whistling Pepper, she led him into the paddock.

Jean waited until Diamond had smelt the halter, then put it on Pepper, and led him around. The mare watched carefully and satisfied herself that there was nothing harmful in this new thing.

Jean approached her, saying softly, " Come on, lady, this is all right. Come on, it won't hurt you." Without any fuss, she slipped the halter on Diamond's sleek neck. The horse trembled all over, but stood quietly while Jean stroked her gently. At the first pull on the rope, however, Black Diamond braced herself and would not budge.

Patiently, Jean coaxed, " Come on, girlie, it's not so bad, really. Come on, you know I wouldn't hurt you."

And then the mare's fear was conquered and she followed obediently, until they had made the rounds of the paddock.

The girl gently removed the halter, and gave both horses some bread. Leaving the gelding and mare, who were now firm friends, Jean literally danced for joy. Black Diamond had sense, that was evident, and the girl raised a song of praise to God in thanks for His help.

After dinner Jean went out again with the halter, and gently put it on the mare. Then she opened the gate, commanded Pepper to follow, and led Diamond out. The mare was nervous at this. She was used to the small paddock, and was distrustful of gates. But her companion was there, Pepper, whose presence never failed to reassure her, encourage her ; and there was Jean's calm voice, coaxing her on. Jean, Diamond knew, was kind and gentle, yet firm, patient, reassuring ; and Jean brought her good things to eat—oats, hay, lucerne, and many titbits. She liked Jean . . . liked everything about her . . . and she wanted to please Jean . . . Diamond went through the gate, and emerged into a wide grassy paddock that spoke of freedom. Black Diamond gave a little jump of excitement.

The saddle horses were grazing peacefully nearby—they were friends—friends that Diamond had longed for in the loneliness of past weeks. And here was grass—rich, green and plentiful ; and a small creek ran through at the eastern end, fed by the melting snows above.

Jean led both horses up and down the paddock, and then removed the halter. Black Diamond was free to do almost as she liked.

" I'll come back tomorrow," Jean told her as she left, " and then I'll take you to see the house, old lady."

At tea, the girl related the incident, winding up in praise of Diamond's sense. " Do you think I could saddle her tomorrow, Dad? " she asked eagerly. But her father thought this inadvisable. " Get her used to the halter first . . . lead her around a bit, and put the saddle on in a couple of days."

Accordingly, the next afternoon, after a short morning storm, Jean haltered Diamond again, led her around the paddock and through the gate nearest the house. Diamond took fright at the strange objects towering above her and around her, but the girl who was so kind, so gentle, patient, and loving, was holding her head and talking quietly to her. The mare knew that Jean would let no harm come to her, so she quietly inspected the buildings, learning that there was nothing of which to be afraid.

" Tomorrow, Diamond," Jean promised as they returned to the paddock, " I'll introduce you to all the people, and the next day, I'll ride you. Oh, Diamond, won't it be lovely, eh? When you and I will explore all the country-side together ! We'll gallop across every plain and jump every creek, won't we, my beautiful pet? " The mare nosed the speaker affectionately, as if she understood the meaning of her words.

Returning to the house, Jean met her father who told her that the brood mares had been sorted out from those who were to be trained. (The stallion had been sold for a very good price some weeks previously.)

" We'll send them out to Charger and start training the others tomorrow. You and Bob and the youngsters can take the mares out now, so run and tell them to come here quickly."

Jean sped off on her mission, and soon four yelling ' demons ', waving arms and cracking stockwhips, drove the few mares and yearlings through gates and fields until the horses had joined Charger's band at the top of a small rise. They left them making acquaintance with the stallion and the station mares.

5

DAWN broke in a vale of pink, red, and gold. A little breeze blew through the open window and fanned Jean's dark hair.

The girl awoke, stretched, gazed out of the window for

a moment, and sprang out of bed. Black Diamond was to be broken in today, and in her morning prayers Jean asked for patience, strength, and skill.

She went to the horse paddock when the milking was completed, and caught the mare. She felt it would have been better to put the saddle on now, while there were no other people to excite Diamond unduly, but it was nearly time for breakfast, so Jean left her with a final caress.

Lessons seemed long and tedious. The geography maps were hard to draw, and the arithmetic sums were on ratio and proportion—the type that Jean hated. However, the books were shelved at last, five minutes before the dinner-bell summoned the household.

The family arranged itself around the table, and Mrs. Brownley said Grace. Jean devoured her meal with such haste that her mother, noting her excitement, chided, " Jean, dear, you'll have awful indigestion if you gobble like that ! " The culprit tried to eat slowly, and accomplished this only with difficulty. At last she put down her pudding spoon, excused herself, and bolted through the door.

" She'll be sick," Mr. Brownley declared, " buck-jumping with a full stomach." His wife went to the door to call Jean back, but the girl had disappeared into the stable to collect saddle and bridle.

" I'd better help her," said Bob, rising, but his father shook his head. " Jean is training this horse . . . she has done it well, so far, and Diamond trusts her so much that I don't think she'll give much trouble ; besides, a stranger will only frighten her more."

Jean approached Black Diamond, and the mare stood quite still until the bridle was put on. She refused, at first, to take the bit into her mouth, for the hard, cold steel bar was foreign to her. At last she submitted, and was led to the breaking-in paddock.

There Jean held the saddle for a while till Diamond had sniffed it well, and finally she put it gently on her back, stroking her and murmuring reassuringly. Diamond was used to a blanket on cold nights, and as Jean tightened the surcingle she merely eyed it enquiringly.

The girl talked quietly to Diamond for some time, stroking her with a firm, kind hand. The mare nuzzled her affectionately, and Jean said smoothly, " Now, old lady, I'm going to ride you. It won't hurt you, girlie, and you'll like it soon. There's no use bucking, 'cause it won't do you any good—it'll only make you feel worse. So don't be frightened, Diamond ; you know I wouldn't hurt you— you trust me, don't you, old girl? "

Then, uttering a prayer for help, Jean gathered the reins and mounted quickly. Once in the saddle, she laid her hand on the horse's neck again, and spoke firmly yet kindly, but Diamond was a brumby, and fear had been part of her natural training. She snorted fiercely, and reared high. Then, tucking her head between her legs, she humped her back, and sprang into the air, landing on stiff forefeet. Twice she repeated this, till Jean was thrown. She got up quickly a little shaken, and caught Black Diamond.

" Silly old girl," she chided, trying to keep that patient, helpful tone, " why ever did you do that? It hasn't got you anywhere, has it? " The girl continued this talk until Black Diamond's nerves were calmed, and finally she said, " Now I'm going to get on you again, so you might as well have some sense and save yourself a lot of bother."

Jean mounted again, but this time the bucking was only half-hearted. Diamond had got over her first fright, and being intelligent, had realized that Jean, who was always kind and loving, would not do anything but for her good. During the previous weeks, Black Diamond had learnt to love the girl who supplied her with food, water, warmth and love and now she felt she would like to obey her.

" Steady, old girl, come on now, steady," Jean pleaded from the saddle, " it's no good bucking. Come on, steady ! " That voice and its owner's presence, that had meant so much to Diamond, now had its effect. Very gradually, the bucking ceased, and the horse stood still, trembling.

Jean flicked the reins over Diamond's shoulders, the mare

started forward, and urged on by her rider made a tour of the paddock.

Halting by the gate, Jean dismounted and removed the saddle. " There ! That wasn't bad, eh, Diamond? " she asked gently. "No reason for all that fuss, was there, old lady? "

Outside, she slipped off the bridle, saying firmly, " Come on, Diamond, come on, girlie." She walked toward the stable, and the mare followed slowly, finding as a reward a delicious carrot. Munching it joyfully, Black Diamond wondered why she had ever refused such a dainty treat. With a final pat and word of praise, Jean turned her loose after rubbing her down, and went over to the house.

" Well," Mrs. Brownley greeted her, " how did you get on? "

" Oh, I got *on* easily, Mother," was the rueful reply, " what I didn't like was the way I got off ! But I've done it ! Black Diamond has got sense, I know, because the second time she only bucked a little, and then stood quiet. And she responded fairly well when I rode her around."

" And what about the first time? " her mother enquired anxiously, " did you hurt yourself when you fell? "

" No, of course not, Mummy darling. You worry an awful lot. I landed on my left hip, and it's still rather tender—but really, I'm as right as rain ; and Diamond was pretty good after the first shock . . . she'll be easy to train, 'cause she's so quick to learn."

In her prayers that night, Jean thanked God for helping her so much, and prayed for more strength for the morrow, when the riding would continue.

Clambering into bed, she went over in her mind the events of the day and of the past weeks. God had answered prayer in sending the brumbies, and He had helped her in training Black Diamond. If only Black Diamond needn't be sold . . . but she was too valuable as a hunter to be kept on the station. Mr. Brownley wouldn't have much use for her, and perhaps it was unfair to spoil a horse's chances like that : yet in her heart, Jean felt that the mare would not be so happy away from the girl she had learned to love. Jean uttered a sigh of mingled happiness and sadness, and fell asleep.

At breakfast next morning Mr. Brownley said, "Jean, when you've finished with Diamond this afternoon, I'll want your help with training the others. We'll run them first, and then show them the hurdles." Jean's eyes danced delightedly, for she revelled in this work.

"We can help, can't we, Dad?" Frank implored, and his father replied, "Yes, son, you two could manage the mares all right now ; they're fairly tame." Margaret rolled her eyes in joyful anticipation, and the youngsters scampered off to do their lessons.

"I'm sick of grammar," grumbled Margaret, shutting a battered exercise-book, "I wish we could be outside with the horses now."

Frank gazed across to the range, and agreed with his sister. "Let's come out and watch them," he suggested with a gleam in his eye, "we'll finish our lessons when we come back." Margaret looked round to where Jean was sitting, her back turned to them, a few yards away. "All right," she murmured, and they tiptoed down the steps and into the small front garden. "If Mother sees us . . ." breathed the boy.

They dodged among wattle and gum trees, describing a wide circle around the house until they reached a point from which the training could easily be seen.

"I wonder if Jean's missing us yet?" said Margaret, as she reached the first bough of a lofty gum.

"Hurry up !" came urgently from below, "here comes Mum !" Frank scrambled up the trunk and together they ascended into the denser upper foliage. "Keep quiet," Frank whispered, "here she is ! Heh ! Mind out—that branch is rotten !"

His sister quickly moved, but it was too late, for as she pushed off to enable her to reach the next bough, the branch snapped and crashed to the ground, just in front of Mrs. Brownley.

She looked up quickly, but could see no one through the canopy of green. Margaret had levered herself to a sitting position, and the pair sat breathlessly peering down. Gum trees are noted for sudden dropping of their limbs, so Mrs. Brownley was not unduly surprised, and passed on.

A sigh of relief escaped both children, and they giggled with relief. Alas, Mrs. Brownley heard the giggles, and immediately turned back.

Closely examining the mass of leaves, she spied a piece of blue—Frank's shirt—and remarked loudly, " My ! I believe I can see Frank's shirt up there ! Now I wonder how it got there ! I'd better go up and get it—it might need washing."

With these words, she clambered up the trunk, agilely for her forty years, but scratching herself a little. " I'm out of practice ! " she scolded herself, and continued her upward journey. " Well I never ! Look at those big cuckoos ! " she exclaimed when she had reached her children. " Are you prospecting for your geography, or trying to get inspiration for your essays ? "

Margaret looked at her brother, and confessed, " We came out to watch the training, and finish our lessons after, Mummy."

" Well," was the understanding reply, " wouldn't it be better to do your lessons first, and get them off your mind? Then you can enjoy yourself all the rest of the day."

So the three scrambled down and the youngsters went back to their lessons to find their sister looking for them.

After dinner, Jean went to the horse paddock with bridle and saddle, and caught Black Diamond. This was an easy task, however, for the mare looked forward to Jean's visits, and sometimes would trot up to her at her call.

Diamond recognized the saddle, but offered no resistance when it was put on. Jean spoke to her for a while, before mounting. When she was in the saddle, however, the mare laid her ears and put her head between her legs, but Jean's voice, commanding, encouraging, and loving, soothed the horse and prevented her from bucking.

Jean flicked the reins, and Diamond cantered slowly along the paddock fence. " Come on, Diamond," she urged, " faster ! " She brushed her shoulders with the reins, half standing up in the stirrups, and her steed quickened her pace, which soon became a gallop.

" Keep it up, old girl," cried Jean, her face aglow. She was amazed at the speed of the mare : Diamond was taking it easily, though the ground was flying beneath her hoofs.

At last, after having circled the paddock for the third time, Jean drew rein and dismounted. She unsaddled the mare, and rubbed her dry before giving her a lump of sugar.

At tea that night, Jean excitedly spoke of Black Diamond's grace and speed ; in fact, she talked of nothing else, except the mare's intelligence. " Tomorrow," she decided, " I'll take her out for a long, steady run, and get her thoroughly used to me and to the saddle, and then I could start training her properly, couldn't I, Dad? "

" Yes, and I think you've done pretty well with her," agreed Mr. Brownley; " you've really trained her already, because now, I believe, she'll obey you in everything." Jean glowed with happiness.

Next day, which was Saturday, the children were freed from their lessons, so Jean decided to take the opportunity to carry some lunch and ride Black Diamond as far as Green Hollow, a valley some distance away, which contained an abundance of rich grass. " We could have lunch there," she thought, " and be back before tea."

So as soon as breakfast was over, and the things had been cleared away, Jean saddled Black Diamond and cantered slowly through the front gate and over Goose Hill, west towards Green Hollow.

She talked gaily as they trotted under the blossoming trees, and Diamond began to enjoy herself. " Come on, girlie, let her go ! " sang Jean, and the mare galloped over an even stretch and slackened near the top of a steep incline.

" Hullo, I wonder who this is? " thought Jean, as a figure on horseback appeared over the brow of the hill.

Black Diamond showed signs of uneasiness, but the girl calmed her and rode towards the newcomer, who proved to be one of their few neighbours, a Mr. Edwards. His face was clouded with anxiety and worry, and approaching Jean he said, " John's lost—near Craggy Hill, I think—he's been gone all night, and we've searched and searched ! "

" I'll help," Jean offered instantly, with the comradeship of the Australian bush ; " which way would be best? "

" Well, we haven't scoured the country south of Craggy Hill yet, so p'r'aps that'd be best."

He galloped off, and the girl turned her mount, remarking, " Well, Diamond, it's up to you . . . you're used to this country." They plunged right into the dense bush, Diamond easily overcoming the many familiar obstacles.

John Edwards, a lad of six, was noted for wandering into the bush, but he had never wandered far, and had always returned to the homestead after a while. ' Perhaps he's hurt,' thought Jean as they cleared a creek, ' hurry, Diamond, oh, hurry ! ' Several times she halted and coo-eed loudly, but only the sighing treetops answered her.

At last, after riding hard for nearly two hours, they reached Craggy Hill, and Jean turned her steed to the left, intending to search south. Zig-zagging at a sharp angle, she probed the thickly-wooded forest, calling loudly, until they emerged into a clearing.

Jean dismounted, ate two sandwiches, for she was ravenous, and Black Diamond started to graze. The girl bit into an apple, and mounted again, deciding to save some of her lunch for John if she should find him.

All afternoon the search continued. Search parties were organized and ceaselessly combed the bush. The Brownleys and other neighbours had been telephoned, and had joined in the hunt.

As the light waned, Jean was sorely tempted to finish her lunch ; Diamond was hungry too, but showed no sign of fatigue. She seemed to sense the urgency, for her splendid pace did not slacken, and her lengthy stride did not shorten.

"Coo-ee!" shouted Jean, almost hoarse now. Suddenly "Coo-ee!" came faintly back to her. For a moment the girl could not believe her ears. "Perhaps it was an echo," she thought, and called again, "Coo-ee! Is that you, John?" A child's sobbing answered her.

Jean's heart leapt, and she cantered quickly in the direction of the sound. Near the base of the hill, she came upon the boy stumbling towards her. As she dismounted, he tripped on a stone and fell, and as Jean ran to pick him up she could see how exhausted and frightened he was. She sat down beside him and gave him the milk she had brought, and the remainder of the sandwiches.

"I'm so hungry!" John sobbed between mouthfuls, "and I'm frikened of the dark, an' I walked for miles an' miles!"

"Poor little laddie!" Jean sympathized as he attacked an orange; "well, home now, eh?"

She lifted him into the saddle, and mounting, wheeled Black Diamond and retraced her steps. For ages, it seemed, they rode on in the dusk, until at last Jean said, "I'm sure I didn't come this way . . . it doesn't look the same." John, overwrought, burst afresh into sobs, and the girl vainly tried to comfort him. "Don't worry, laddie; I'll get you out of this."

She dismounted, and went to Diamond's head, saying desperately, "Black Diamond, you know where your home is; take us there. It's up to you, old lady. Come on, you'll take us home, won't you, girlie?" She looked into the mare's intelligent eyes, and felt some satisfaction in what she saw.

She mounted and lightly flicked the reins across Diamond's shoulders, commanding, "Home, Diamond, quickly!"

The mare pricked her ears, and started forward, obedient to Jean's word and touch. The track she took was strange to Jean, and often the girl wondered if Diamond was heading in the right direction. "O God," she prayed, "guide Black Diamond and keep us safe!"

Diamond gathered speed as if she knew she was nearing her destination, and Jean's faith in the mare increased as steadily as did the pace.

John was dozing as he rode, leaning hard on Jean, whose back began to ache. She was feeling desperately hungry, and her task of cheering the wanderer was difficult.

It seemed they had ridden for hours when Jean sighted familiar landmarks, and they left the bush for a clearing not far from the station gate. "Black Diamond!" cried Jean as she raised thanks to God. "You've done it! I knew you would!" However, she found the homestead deserted except for Margaret and Frank, who greeted them with cries of relief, and explained that the others had formed another search party. Jean left them to telephone the various homes, telling the glad news, while she gave John some food, and then put him to bed.

Mrs. Edwards came hurrying across to collect her son, but spent the night with the Brownleys in order to give John a good spell of sleep. Next day, overflowing with gratitude to Jean and Black Diamond, she carried the wanderer home.

Jean had retold the adventures of the day around the supper table, praising Diamond's intelligence and stamina, and during family prayers hearts were raised to God in thankfulness for safe delivery of John and Jean.

6

JEAN awoke one fine spring morning to the gay songs of the many different mountain birds. She looked happily out of the window on to the sunlit range, and realized that it was time for Black Diamond to be put over the hurdles.

Before the milking she whistled the mare and rode her around bareback. She seldom used Pepper now, for Diamond needed all the attention and training she could give. Besides, Pepper was really past retiring age, and lacked the mare's strength and speed.

A mist was rising from the valleys as Jean unbridled her steed—a typical mountain mist, wrapping the hills in a ghostly shroud, and shutting out the daylight everywhere lower than the lofty peaks.

" It's a morning mist," Jean remarked to herself, and she was right, for as she ploughed through her geometry the cloudy veil was lifting, and by midday a clear blue sky and warm sun had taken the place of the damp grey atmosphere.

Jean ran lightly into the horse paddock after dinner with saddle and bridle, and whistled Black Diamond, riding her to a large field where were an assortment of hurdles, all different sizes and shapes.

Being used to the rough, uneven ground of the trackless mountain scrub—the home of the brumbies—Black Diamond was surefooted and used to jumping, and took the hurdles as a matter of course. She needed little urging on Jean's part ; she seemed to like jumping, and Jean was thrilled at the graceful ease with which Diamond sailed over the hurdles.

The girl gave her a spell, and then galloped up to the high fences. Diamond jumped these with no apparent effort, until finally they approached the last and highest— almost the same height as the fence which the mare had jumped months ago, when she had been the embodiment of fear and angry skill. Diamond gathered herself and sprang, clearing the top bar with inches to spare, even with Jean's weight to hamper her. The girl drew rein and dismounted, deciding that it was better to make haste slowly.

" Good old lady," she praised the horse, as she led her back to the horse paddock. " You did very well, girlie ; I'm proud of you, and you'll make a name for yourself yet ! " A pang shot through her heart at her own words, as she realized that she would never know what was to happen to Diamond when she was sold. The bitter thought made her rebellious. Suppose Black Diamond did become famous—it would be mostly through Jean, and no one would ever know of the patient, loving work they had shared together, the hours that had been spent in training. Oh, why did Diamond have to be sold? With all the horses on the station, couldn't her father spare one from the sales? Jean sighed, fondly smoothing Diamond's mane, before she hastened to help with the other mares.

The brumbies were all good jumpers, though none came up to Black Diamond, for the horses, when running through the bush, would have to overcome many obstacles in the shape of creeks and fallen logs.

A few of the mares had already been put over the low hurdles in the preceding days, while others were still being ridden around to acquaint them thoroughly with the saddle.

" Which one shall I take, Dad? " called Jean as she approached the hurdle paddock again.

" That cream one's ready," answered Mr. Brownley. Jean mounted the saddled horse and cantered slowly to the first jump, not much more than two feet high. The cream took it familiarly, and completed the set of six low jumps. This performance was repeated several times, and the mare was then shown the higher fences.

Margaret and Frank were working hard on two bay colts, believed to be twins. All the station hands were fully occupied with the horses, and the training ground was a hive of activity. Jean was enjoying herself immensely, for she was in her element when dealing with horses. Bob had been busy all day, riding and jumping the mares. There were twelve mares and nineteen yearlings that Mr. Brownley thought worth training: the remainder of the mares would help to make up for the loss in the brood mares.

By evening the workers were glad to leave their task for tea, for training means concentration and long hours in the saddle.

" Did you see Black Diamond clear the last hurdle? " Jean asked eagerly. " I thought she would, but I was surprised at the way she took it."

" Yes, all this herd seems to regard the fences as old friends," Mr. Brownley remarked. " It's a good thing," his wife put in, " they'll make good hunters, and they're in demand now. I believe this band will help us a lot, financially."

" I think Diamond's about the best jumper, though," said Bob, " and she's so powerful and quick ! " Jean revelled in this praise of her darling, and grinned at her brother almost gratefully.

That night the workers slept that deep, healthy sleep which follows long and tiring work in the open, and in the morning they were as fresh as ever.

The youngsters finished their lessons nearly an hour before dinner, and thankfully forsook the verandah for the training paddock.

" Oh, boy ! Look at this ! " Margaret exclaimed, stopping near the incinerator. She picked up a broken lens out of the rubbish, and Frank joyfully chimed in, " A magnifying glass ! " For a time, the horses were forgotten, as the pair retraced their steps to the house, the girl clutching her prize.

Ever since Bob had shown them how to burn their initials on paper with a magnifying glass they had longed to do it, but the glass had been lost, and their opportunity as well. Now the precious lens had been found, and entering the house, Frank seized a newspaper (unfortunately, that day's paper) and ran off to the stable to indulge in a favourite pastime.

" I'm doing mine first ! " Margaret commanded, and sat patiently holding the glass in a position for throwing the rays of the sun on the paper. Presently the paper began to smoulder. Very slowly, Margaret moved the glass, until a line of burnt paper, resembling an " M ", resulted. Then a " B " was formed, and Frank took over, remarking, " You forgot to put in the full stops." He laboriously burnt out " F.B. ", and suggested, " Let's do sentences now ! "

Margaret seized the paper, took a clean sheet, and after some time, " YOU ARE MAD " was written across the page. Frank returned this insult with his sentence, " DITTO PIGTAILS ". Now, if there was anything that Margaret hated, it was to be called ' pigtails ', and Frank felt fully compensated as he saw her face. Thus the game went on, until most of the newspaper had gone up in smoke.

The dinner bell sounded, and the youngsters answered gladly, forsaking all for a piping hot meal. Bob was attacking his mutton when he remarked, " I can smell smoke or something."

" I can smell something burning, too," Mrs. Brownley joined in. She glanced through the open doorway, and gasped, " The stable's on fire ! "

The family rushed out, meeting the men who were running from their quarters. Mr. Brownley rushed to an underground tank, and threw off the lid, shouting " Bucket ! " This was rather unnecessary, however, for all the buckets had been gathered, and another tank opened.

With all the speed they could muster they filled everything available with water, and emptied it on and around the burning stable.

The flames were licking the walls, climbing higher and higher, until they had nearly reached the roof. The fire-fighters worked desperately, choking and blinded by smoke, eyes smarting and backs aching. Fortunately, all the horses were out in the paddock, but the hay was highly inflammable, and the fire raged inside and out.

For nearly an hour they fought the menacing flames, and eventually they triumphed. The fire was quelled, and the curtain of smoke lifted.

The stable presented a sorry sight, charred and streaming with water. The Brownleys inspected the damage, which, because of the stone floor and partly stone walls, was remarkably slight. The woodwork would have to be replaced, likewise the mangers and stalls. Some of the feed had disappeared, but there was still enough to last for a good while, as the room was well stocked.

They emerged from the reeking stable, and surveyed one another in the sunlight. Their faces and hands were black, and their eyes bloodshot and watery. A sense of humour came to their aid, and they laughed at the comical sight they presented.

" How did it happen? " wondered Jean, and the others echoed her question. Nobody seemed to know the answer. And then Frank spied the remains of the magnifying glass. It was lying on the ground where the newspaper and a small pile of hay had once been. " Margaret ! " he cried with horror, " it must have been the glass ! " The young-sters stood rooted to the spot as the outcome of their care-lessness dawned upon them.

" What glass? " demanded the company.

" This magnifying glass," Margaret jerked as she picked it up. She dropped it quickly, for it was almost red hot, and she explained shakily, " We were burning paper with it ! "

Jaws dropped and eyes bulged at her words !

" My fault," Bob shrugged, " I showed them how to do it. I s'pose I should have had more sense ! "

" No, it's our fault," Frank protested despairingly, and Margaret joined in, " We were careless, leaving it there . . . and Mum's always telling me I should be more careful ! "

The youngsters were looking repentantly sorrowful, not for any punishment they expected to receive, but for the calamity they had brought about. Mrs. Brownley felt more pity than anger as she looked at her children's doleful faces, and decided that the punishment they were suffering would be enough to teach them a lesson. Her husband's thoughts were similar, and he merely said, " Oh, well, it could have been worse ; it might have been the house. You two had better remember, in future, to think twice before you act."

He strode away to wash and finish dinner, and the others followed suit, relieved. Mrs. Brownley never lectured them, but was not past giving a short word of advice. She laid her hand on the youngsters' shoulders and looked at them kindly, saying, " *Do* try to be more careful, children ! " She smiled and went inside, and the pair followed gratefully.

Once again the family sat down around the table, this time to a cold, greasy dinner. " I'll put these in the oven," Mrs. Brownley offered, but this raised an outcry, for the family firmly declared itself too hungry to wait for dinner to be heated.

The following day, Mr. Brownley commenced to repair the damage as far as possible. Margaret and Frank worked extra hard on the stable, under their father's supervision, clearing up the result of their carelessness. All afternoon they worked, while Mr. Brownley and the men sawed and drilled, fitted and nailed. Bob and Jean placed the fodder in the sun to dry, and rearranged the chaotic stalls, and by evening the stable looked little worse for its adventure.

At tea Bob suggested a shooting expedition while daylight lasted. Margaret and Frank accepted readily, and as soon as the jobs were done, they shouldered rifles and

sacks and turned toward Craggy Hill, a favourite hunting
ground.

"Better not go too far," advised Jean, "this place is
simply wicked when you're lost."

Bob grinned at her and taunted, "The wisdom of the
experienced!" They walked along in the dusk, teasing
each other and shooting an occasional rabbit.

Meanwhile, in the homestead, quietness reigned—a
change from the noisy presence of the children.   Mr.
Brownley stretched comfortably on the verandah couch,
while his wife mended industriously.

"I don't know what to do about those children," said
the father, "always up to something, and never two things
alike."

"Oh, they'll come out all right.   Bob and Jean were the
same—in fact, they're still pretty mischievous at times."

"Not so bad as the youngsters, though.   I suppose they
just can't help it—and we can't stop them, either."

"They're not really bad," Mrs. Brownley countered,
thoughtfully, "only careless, and rather thoughtless, too."

"Yes ; they don't mean any harm, really, and they're
quite good-hearted.   But I wish . . . oh, I suppose we were
worse when we were kids!"

Meantime the younger Brownley members were trekking
gaily through the scrub, joking to and about each other,
and whistling snatches of a song.

"We'll frighten all the rabbits, making all this row!"
reproved Bob, and Jean let a long low whistle escape her.
"My hat!" she breathed, "you're the rowdiest of us all :
you can't get away with that!"

Before she had finished the sentence Jean stopped, lifted
her rifle into position, and fired.   A small grey ball of fur
dropped lifeless, and the shooter went forward to examine
her prize.   The skins added to their pocket money, and the
flesh made tasty meals.

Bob saw a movement some yards away, and fired,
aiming accurately at a large brown rabbit.   "Two caught
in five minutes . . . that's good!"

The sun was slowly sinking nearer the western horizon, and he added, " We'd better go home now . . . we mustn't be caught here in the dark." So the party made its way to the homestead, shooting occasionally as they walked.

Suddenly Jean saw something move among the shadows. She couldn't quite see what it was, but presuming it to be a rabbit, she raised her gun and took careful aim.

Bang! A sharp cry of pain followed the report, and the four stared at each other before hurrying forward to investigate. What they saw made them gasp and whiten, for Jean's target was a man.

7

"IS he dead?" Margaret cried out, almost hysterical.

Bob, unflurried as usual, bent down and examined the man, finally commenting, " No, fainted. It looks as if some of the shot stuck together and went into his stomach." With dexterity that astonished the children, he tied a stone in his handkerchief, and strapped it to the wound with the man's belt, to prevent bleeding.

" Who is he? " wondered Jean. " I've never seen him before."

" Looks like a stranger," commented Bob, " p'r'haps a visitor, lost in the bush."

" He's terribly thin," Jean put in, " he looks starved and ill."

The man rallied slightly, opened his eyes for a moment, and groaned. " Steady, old chap," murmured Bob.

Under his bushy beard was the face of a young man : his clothes were in shreds, and his skin dirty . . . an odd man, who presented a rather gruesome sight. He opened his eyes again and muttered incoherently.

" We'll have to get him home quickly. Shirt and coat,
Frank," Bob ordered, and soon an impromptu stretcher
was ready for the patient. Jogging him as little as possible,
they moved him by this means out of the dense bush,
towards the homestead.

At the gate, Mr. Brownley saw them and came to investigate. His wife hurried inside to boil some water and
prepare bandages and rugs. The man was laid gently on
the sofa, and given a cup of hot, sweet, black tea. That
seemed to do him good, for he rallied a little from his
stupor. " Where am I? " he asked, bewildered.

" You were shot in the stomach," Mr. Brownley informed
him, " and we're going to look after you till you're better."
The man, exhausted, sank into a coma.

Although the three were bursting with curiosity, they
left him in peace, and went quietly to bed. Mrs. Brownley
'phoned Doctor Rex, who promised to come quickly. " I
don't think it's a very bad wound," Bob remarked, as he
placed a clean dressing in position. He longed to extract
the embedded shot himself, instead of waiting for Doctor
Rex, but lacking equipment, he was forced to leave the
patient as he was.

Doctor Rex arrived at last with anaesthetic and instru-
ments. Bob hovered around and eventually asked, " Could
I help you with the anaesthetic? I've learned a bit about
it." The doctor, somewhat naturally, refused, but Bob
implored again. Doctor Rex looked beyond him to Mrs.
Brownley, and raised a questioning eyebrow. The mother,
remembering Dick Harris's leg, and the medical journals
on the bedroom bookcase, nodded.

Bob swung round and saw the nod. He flashed a grateful
grin and unhesitatingly set about his task.

Doctor Rex was amazed at the knowledge the boy dis-
played. The operation was soon completed, and the small
lump of shot removed.

" It's not very serious," was the doctor's diagnosis ; " all
you have to do now is keep his dressings clean, and he'll be
better in a month."

The family filed on to the verandah to see Doctor Rex depart.

"Someone will have to watch him until he comes round," was his last injunction, "and by the way, Bob, you managed pretty well. Wherever did you glean all your knowledge? "

Bob flushed with pleasure, and murmured, "Oh, I've just read it in books and things."

Doctor Rex made little effort to conceal his puzzlement. "Well, you helped me a great deal," were his last words. "Goodbye, everybody ! "

Mrs. Brownley accompanied him a little way to where his horse was tethered. "Doctor," she began, "Bob's very keen to take up the medical profession. He has scores of books and journals in his room, and I think he reads them at night. He doesn't tell anyone, because he knows that we can't spare the money for his training. What would the cost be, roughly? "

"About £2,000."

Mrs. Brownley shrugged her shoulders, but Doctor Rex continued, "Mrs. Brownley, we must pray about it. I'm glad you told me, for now I can give you my support."

"Thank you, awfully. I know Bob prays about it, and I do, too. God will clear the way, if it's His will. Well, goodbye, Doctor."

The doctor cantered towards the gate, and Mrs. Brownley hurried back to the house, where Bob was feeling the patient's pulse.

"I'll stay with him," volunteered his mother, who was a good nurse, and the others went to the paddocks to continue their afternoon work.

The patient spent a feverish night, but the next day he had recovered from the effects of the anaesthetic, and was looking wearily about him. His pain was somewhat better, and he was able to talk a little.

"What's your name? " Mr. Brownley asked.

"Joe Wood."

"Have you come far? "   "Where are you making for? "

Joe was very evasive in his answers. The family thought

talking had tired him, for he lay back on the pillow and was soon asleep again . . . yet not so soundly as to miss altogether the murmur of Mr. Brownley's voice as he read the Bible and prayed at the family prayers.

Joe recorded the fact with distaste. ' Ugh ! Bible-punchers ! Just my luck ! As if I hadn't had enough of this stuff ! Guess they'll preach to me and give me tracts and more tracts. I'll get out of here as soon as I can.' Then he fell asleep again more soundly.

He was roused later by Bob, who inspected the dressing on his wound, and decided to change it, making it comfortable for the night. The man at first doubted the ability of the boy, but soon realized that his youth did not mean lack of skill.

Mrs. Brownley, in her tenderest tones, coaxed Joe to have a little beef tea—and such delicious beef tea, too. " It will keep you going till morning," she said, " I shall sleep better if I know you are not hungry." In spite of himself, Joe felt a glow of warm comfort from Mrs. Brownley's motherly concern for him. He took the proffered nourishment with eagerness.

Mrs. Brownley smiled at him and said, " That's good to see. I can tell you will be a good patient. I feel we are going to enjoy your forced stay with us. Goodnight, Joe, God bless you."

Only a grunt escaped Joe's lips. What more could these folk have done for him? This cosy kitchen, this soft clean bed, this boy so attentive, this tender, womanly care ; never had he dreamed that all this would be his lot.

Mrs. Brownley rigged up a camp bed in the kitchen for Bob, knowing he would not be content to be too far from the patient. She knew her son was living his dreams, and left Joe confidently to his care.

Except for a few fitful mutterings, Joe slept all night. Although the family came to breakfast quietly next morning, Joe was awake, so they showered him with enquiries after his health.

The patient felt better, and was able to eat the light

breakfast served daintily to him by Mrs. Brownley. The family 'Grace' aroused his suspicion. He expected the 'preaching' to start any moment, and was prepared with his answer. It did not come, however, so he settled back to rest again.

Jean ploughed through her lessons that morning, and completed them before twelve o'clock. She dashed out to the hurdle paddock, where she was met by Bob, who had just taken the high jumps on Sugar, the quietest mare. " This horse will be excellent for a lady's or child's hunter," he remarked, " a fairly good jumper, and sweet-natured."

Jean saddled a chestnut and put her through her paces. At the highest jump the mare baulked, and Jean was thrown over the fence. She knew how to fall, however, and so was not injured. They tried again, and this time the chestnut knocked the top bar down. Jean kept her at jumping the lower hurdles until dinner time, and then she showed her the high fence again. The mare just managed to clear it, but Jean could tell from the effort put forth that she was not a good high jumper.

Beside high jumping there was long jumping, such as the water jump, and Mr. Brownley decided to try the mares at those in the afternoon.

Bob changed Joe's dressing, noting that the wound was clean, and no complications had arisen. The boy was in his element when tending the patient. Since Joe had come into the home, something new had entered Bob's life and taken possession of him. A new desire had seized his mind, though he could not quite grasp it in solid form. It puzzled and worried him, for Bob was very practical and not usually subject to shallow emotions, and this feeling that could not be expressed, even to his mother or Jean, was strange to him. Bob pinned the bandage and hurried out to join the others.

The creek which wound through the station property served excellently for training horses for long jumps, as it varied greatly in width.

" May I start on Black Diamond, Dad? " asked Jean.

"Yes, but don't forget the others must be done, will you, Jeanie?" Mr. Brownley grinned as his daughter ran off to bring Black Diamond. "It's easy to see she's crazy over that mare," he remarked to Bob.

It was nothing new for Jean to be 'crazy' over a horse —she was really 'crazy' over them all. But Black Diamond was different. Between the two had sprung up more than a friendship—it was a deep, strong understanding and affection.

Jean saddled Black Diamond, and rode her towards the Swagman, where the creek wound narrowly from the mountains. "Come on, Diamond, old girl, this is easy," encouraged Jean, and the mare flew over the water with her customary graceful ease. This was repeated a few times, and then Jean praised Diamond and took her a little way downstream to a wider section.

Fifty yards away, Mr. Brownley was supervising the training of the other horses, which were progressing rapidly.

Black Diamond cleared the stream easily, and after a time Jean took her farther to a very broad stretch of water. "Now, Diamond, you can do this, too," Jean urged, "come on, over we go!"

The mare leapt into the air and landed on the opposite bank, and the watchers gasped at this display of equestrian skill.

"Good old lady! I knew you could do it! You're marvellous, Diamond!" Diamond gave a little snort, just as if she completely understood the praise.

Jean worked on the horse for some time before turning her into the paddock. The day was pleasantly warm, with light breezes rustling in the tree tops and fanning the hot cheeks of the workers.

Watching Mrs. Brownley busy in her kitchen, so bright, so considerate of him, Joe began to feel less bitter, less hostile. Soon she began to attract him—he began to feel glad he was in her presence and a new kind of peace began to steal into his heart.

After a while, Margaret and Frank came in to look at

Joe. " Well, young 'uns," the latter said, " what have you been up to all afternoon? "

" Training the horses for long jumping," Margaret replied.

" Let's hope there won't be any more mischief from you two," smiled Mrs. Brownley, " we've had all we want, haven't we, Joe? "

The man felt drawn into the family circle by this remark : it was a pleasant feeling, too, and it struggled with his decision to ' get out as soon as possible '.

The conversation was interrupted by the entrance of the rest of the family in response to the tea bell. " Well, Joe, how are things? " Mr. Brownley enquired heartily.

" Not bad, Boss," was the reply, and the same feeling of uneasiness began to arise within him.

Bob seemed to make a bee-line for the patient in a quite professional manner, while Mr. and Mrs. Brownley glanced at each other almost despairingly, and from each heart a silent prayer was raised that God would open the way for Bob's training. " Quite comfy, Joe? " Bob asked.

Joe's heart struggled again with conflicting emotions. He must get away from this Bible-punching, Grace-saying family, yet what a fool he'd be to leave such a friendly, jolly home as this ! Why, they could even be loving him, the way they treated him. Love ! When did he ever know love? Could he hurry away? Yes, he must, before they found out what he was, and why he had been where he was when the youngster shot him. However, for the present, he would enjoy all they liked to give him, and pretend to take in the ' preaching '.

Sunday dawned, and Joe steeled his heart with stronger bands against the expected ' preaching '. ' I s'pose they'll go round reading the Bible an' singing hymns all day,' he thought morosely.

At the breakfast table, Mrs. Brownley said, " I'll stay home with Joe—that is, if he doesn't mind my company ! " She laughed, and Joe murmured a denial, cheerily enough, but inwardly writhing at this supposed promise of a lecture.

Bob replaced the hard, soiled dressing with a clean, soft swab of cotton wool and lint, and announced that the wound was healing nicely. By this time, it was just after half-past nine, and a merry crowd gathered at the front of the house with their horses to bid farewell.

Through the open kitchen window, Joe surveyed them in wonderment. This ' religious lot ' was actually gay and jolly on *Sunday*, and by their happy faces one could almost imagine they enjoyed going to church. Where was all the long-faced piety that Bible-punchers usually put on when they were going to listen to a sermon? Joe could not understand this apparent contradiction of his former impressions.

Mrs. Brownley prepared a tasty dinner, talking happily of this and that, and sometimes joking with the patient, who once more felt drawn out of his bitterness, and occasionally joined in with a hearty laugh or comment. Mrs. Brownley noted this, and praised God.

The day was warm and sunny, and when the chicken was safely in the oven, Mrs. Brownley said, " Joe, would you like to go out on the verandah in the sun? I think it would do you good."

" Yes, thank you, missus," was the thankful reply, " if you don't mind."

Mrs. Brownley wheeled the heavy couch to a position from which Joe could survey his surroundings on three sides, with his head in the shade and his body in the sun. Grateful for the penetrating warmth, the man tried stretching luxuriously, only to find that this hurt his stomach.

Mrs. Brownley came out with a table, chair, and stationery, remarking, as she put these in place, " Dinner's not ready yet, so I'll write a few letters. I get awfully behind with my correspondence if I don't keep hard at it ! " He laughed with her ; it was almost impossible not to be in sympathy with that jolly, understanding mother.

" Would you like something to read, Joe? " she enquired, after a while. " I'm afraid I'm dooming you to a state of boredom."

" Oh, no, thanks, missus ; I'm all right." Joe's answer was hasty, for he dreaded her giving him the inevitable tracts and texts. And then, so as not to seem ungrateful, he added, " I just like looking at the view." Joe was suspicious of Mrs. Brownley's every action until she had quite settled to her writing.

The sun beamed down and seemed to pour health into the sick man, for his face relaxed, he became drowsy, and presently drifted into sleep.

Some time later, Mrs. Brownley woke him with a dainty tray bearing an appetising meal of chicken and peas, followed by a tasty blancmange. They ate it together, Mrs. Brownley saying a short but reverent Grace, which put Joe on the alert again.

Having washed up, Mrs. Brownley settled down to read some church papers, in which she quickly became absorbed.

Joe went over in his mind the events of the day—the tender care and thoughtfulness that had been his lot—and he felt gratitude rising up within him. He longed to satisfy his curiosity in many things, and this homely woman was the right person in whom to confide.

A battle raged in Joe's heart until finally he burst forth, " Missus, do you have a good time at church? "

Mrs. Brownley's heart leapt, for this was the opening she had prayed for. " My word, yes, Joe ! I think it's great ! "

" What do you do there? "

" Well, we sing hymns and read the Bible, and then Mr. Marsh talks to us about God and His Word. We always enjoy it thoroughly ! "

Joe lay back, and turned his head. Sing hymns ! Read the Bible ! Listen to a long sermon ! The very thought of it filled him with horror. But these people liked it ! And they were always happy. They were a heap happier than he . . . but then, they were a lot better off. Joe was still puzzled, and ventured to ask no more questions.

Late in the afternoon the family returned, and, in tones that were anything but solemn, passed on scraps of the sermons, and news of the neighbours.

Joe was wheeled inside, and Bob changed his dressing again. During family prayers after tea the man watched attentively, and could see no pious gloom registered on the faces of the listeners. "It's funny," he mused, "there's something about them: I wonder what it is?"

8

"YES, and then we dressed up in sheets, and pretended to be ghosts!" "And didn't we scare them! And we explored the cave when we'd finished our supper!" The youngsters had just stacked away the lesson books, and were animatedly telling Joe the story of a midnight feast in Ghost Cavern.

"And we drank toasts, and when we'd finished, Bob pretended to be crazy!" "Oh-h-h! It was awful creepy inside the cave. We were going to tell each other ghost stories, but we were too scared!"

Joe chuckled as he listened.

"Go and wash your hands, children," came Mrs. Brownley's voice from the kitchen, "and then bring Joe inside."

The patient spent his days on the verandah now, in a different place every day, so that his view would not become monotonous, and the sun, the greatest of healers, shone its rays on to him, and soaked him through and through, pouring new life into him.

The dinner bell rang, and Mr. Brownley, followed by his elder children, entered the room, chatting and laughing.

"Ned Gilmore promised me that equipment I lent him weeks ago," he said during the course of the meal. "Jean, you could ride over this afternoon and get it. Black Diamond needs more exercise."

"Oh, good, Dad! I'll take Diamond over some fences on the way."

So when the meal was finished, Jean caught Black Diamond, and led her to the stable to be bridled and saddled.

Mrs. Brownley and Joe waved goodbye from the verandah. "It's wonderful, the way she can manage that mare," remarked Joe, who seemed to be particularly interested in the horses.

"Yes," Mrs. Brownley replied. "She possesses some peculiar power over animals: some people have it, and they're very fortunate."

Black Diamond cantered down the track to the front gate, nearly half a mile away, and sailed over the gate at Jean's bidding. The hoofs thudded a jogging rhythm on the dusty track as Diamond trotted steadily downwards. The mountain horses—those born and bred there—are very surefooted, and the mare proved to be no exception as she turned and twisted among trees and rocks that obstructed the unkept path.

The morning had been hot, but now a breeze rustled the tree-tops, steadily gaining force until it whistled and shrieked through the gums, and shook their branches. Jean shivered slightly and urged Diamond on, for they were in danger of falling branches in this gale.

They fought on against the head wind, until they had

neared their destination, when Diamond suddenly stopped, almost shooting Jean over her head.

" Go on, old lady.   We can't stay in this place too long ! Go on, Diamond ! "

But for once the mare was disobedient.   She snorted and tossed her head.   " What's wrong, girlie?   Go on, hurry ! " Diamond held her ground against kicks and slaps, and Jean, with her knowledge of animals, sensed danger ahead. She dismounted and went to Diamond's head.

C-r-r-rack !   Not three yards in front of the pair, a rotten yet heavy bough burst through the foliage and crashed to the ground.

Diamond started violently, but Jean calmed her with voice and hand.   " Good girl ! " she praised with fervour. " O, God, thank you so much ! "

They leapt the bough and continued their journey, soon arriving at Gilmore's farm.

Jack and Teddy, the two sons, were walking towards the front gate, and hailed Jean eagerly.   " I've come over for those tools Dad lent your father," Jean explained at length, after they had chatted for some time.

" Oh, yes," replied ten-year-old Jack, " Dad's got them ready.   Come and get 'em."

Jean dismounted, and the three walked towards the bungalow, Black Diamond following Jean, a little distrustful of the boys.   " That mare's bonza," remarked Teddy, two years younger than Jack.   " Of course she is," was the proud answer, " she follows me around now."   The boys admired her perfect build and carriage, asking many questions about her.

Approaching the front verandah, they were greeted by Mrs. Gilmore, herself an ardent horse-lover, who fell to praising the beautiful black mare before she even asked the reason for Jean's visit.

" I've come for the tools," the girl said, after a while, and Mrs. Gilmore instantly replied, " Oh, yes, Mr. Gilmore left them here in this box, ready for you.   Your father said someone would call for them this week."

She handed Jean the heavy box, remarking, "You'll have to go slow with that, dear." They chatted on for a little while, and Jean related the recent incident, but Diamond grew restless, so the girl mounted and started on her homeward journey.

The wind had not abated, and Jean shivered as she rode through the gate. They retraced their steps along the dangerous track, the cumbersome box reducing their speed. Diamond wound in and out at a swinging trot, dropping into a walk where the incline was severe.

At last, after almost two hours of this, they climbed the steepest slope, and halted before the gate of the mountain home. Jean opened it, and rode toward the house, where she was welcomed by Mrs. Brownley and Joe.

"Well, how was Diamond?" Joe asked, "did she behave?"

Jean laughed as she answered, "Behave! She was marvellous. And what do you think? We were nearly at Gilmore's, when Diamond stopped suddenly, and wouldn't budge. I tried to make her go on, but she wouldn't, and then a huge branch broke off the tree in front of us, and it would have hit us hard, but for Diamond!"

The listeners paid tribute to the horse with silent admiration. Mrs. Brownley had read things like that in books; but in reality . . . oh, well! she might have known Black Diamond would do a thing like that!

Jean carried the box inside, and rode to the horse paddock. Her errand had taken up most of the afternoon, so she decided against joining the workers. "I'll groom Diamond; she certainly needs it," she thought as she turned the mare's head back towards the stable.

Black Diamond stood patiently while her young mistress rubbed her down, dusted her, brushed her, and combed her mane and tail. The busy stationers had little time to spare from the work, and so jobs like this had to be done in odd moments.

Around the dinner table, Jean retold her adventure colourfully. The memory of it was vivid; apart from the wonderful escape from injury or death, it had been one more proof of God's loving protection, and also of Black Diamond's sense. It seemed to Jean that the incidents that had occurred in connection with Diamond were important, as if leading up to something. The involuntary love for each other, the understanding between them, the times they had shared, the realization of Jean's dreams, the answer to prayer—surely not to be shattered by a blow of the auctioneer's hammer!

Jean sighed deeply as she spread her bread liberally with jam and cream. In prayers, Mr. Brownley read that portion of the Epistle to the Romans which includes the verse, "All things work together for good to them that love God, to them who are the called according to His purpose," and Jean knew that God would order all things well for His child.

Next morning, Bob awoke early, and after dressing, went outside to drink in the fresh morning air. Passing through the kitchen, he glanced at Joe, and as he did so the un-formed feeling within him grew till he felt he could not contain himself. He strove to discover what it was that made his heart burn with longing. And then, like a flash, it dawned upon his puzzled brain. A medical missionary! That's what he was meant to be! Not only to heal broken bodies, but to mend broken souls. Tending Joe for the past days had awakened in Bob this new desire ; he, by studying, had helped to heal Joe's wound, but . . . what about his soul? The boy gasped as he realized the truth —and at that moment Joe roused.

"Oh, good morning!" greeted Bob, "I'm going out to have a breather . . . wish you could come?"

"Ummm!" the patient murmured sleepily.

Bob laughed and opened the door, making a bee-line for a paddock where the cows were grazing. He rounded them up and brought them in, and all the time his mind was occupied with the feeling which had so recently become clear. It raged like a fever within him, and refused to be banished.

Breakfast was a merry affair, as everyone, for no particular reason, was in high spirits. " I think we'd better look over the herd," instructed Mr. Brownley, meaning Charger and the brood mares, " we'll have to bring them in soon, and sort out the yearlings."

" Can we come? " The question rose involuntarily to the lips of the youngsters, but their wish could not be granted. " You have your lessons to do," Mr. Brownley reminded them, " and you'd only get excited, and frighten the mares. No, I'm sorry ; wait till you're older, and then we'll see."

The children were crestfallen as Jean asked eagerly if she could go with her father and Bob. Mr. Brownley looked at his elder daughter and said, " You have your lessons, too, Jean. You can see the horses any time when you're riding out that way."

So, after the meal, Bob followed his father to the horse paddock, where they saddled their mounts and cantered towards the Swagman, where Charger was guarding his band.

" When are we going to bring them in, Dad? " Bob asked, as the horses paced through a narrow gully.

" Oh, if possible, I'd like to get them in some time next week. Let's see . . . this is Friday . . ." he pondered for a while, " . . . . we shall round them up next Wednesday."

" We might have some trouble with the brumbies," Bob remarked, and his father grinned. " Then we'll have to do it in the afternoon, so that Jean can help—she'll be in seventh heaven ! "

Under boughs and over logs the horses made their way onwards and upwards, until the Swagman loomed nearby and cast its shadow over the riders. Quietly they proceeded, taking every precaution against scaring the half-wild horses.

" We ought to see them soon," Mr. Brownley murmured, and he proved to be right, for, rounding a hillock, they looked over the edge of a steep precipice into a valley liberally spread with fresh green grass, where the mares, foals, and yearlings were grazing peacefully.

The black stallion, Charger, had sensed the presence of the men, and was eyeing them from a mound some distance beneath them. Between the station owner and the horse existed a perfect understanding ; it was as if they ran the station together, and now they were consulting with each other. Bob looked on in silence and a little awe ; this spectacle never failed to fill watchers with wonder.

From the edge of the cliff, they surveyed the herd, which numbered twenty-three mares, as many yearlings, and nearly as many foals. " Four of them haven't foaled yet," Mr. Brownley commented, " they're nearly overdue."

The two lingered there for a moment, noting the condition of the horses, who had recently come through another trying winter, when the wind and rain had chilled their bodies, and the grass had disappeared under a cold mantle of snow. " Ginger won't last another winter," said Bob, naming the oldest mare, " but the others have pulled through all right."

The horses completed a picturesque scene as they cropped the grass against a background of rugged, snow-capped mountains and vivid green herbage, crowned with a deep blue sky from where the sun beamed its generous warmth over all the countryside.

Ginger was dozing, while her cream filly frisked and frolicked with her playmates. Bouncer was licking her new-born roan, whose legs were rather shaky ; and there was Sooty with a savage-looking colt, and many others with a wide variety of colour and nature.

" We'd better go back now," Mr. Brownley urged after a while. Father and son rode homewards happily, in eager anticipation of the Wednesday to come, for all the family had a taste for excitement and adventure.

Meeting Jean, whose lessons were completed, Bob passed on the good news. This resulted in a yell as the girl performed a war-dance on the spot—which happened to be the back verandah. " Jean, whatever is the matter? "

asked Mrs. Brownley, as she investigated, " the house will collapse in a minute ! " Her ruffian daughter laughed gaily as she cried, " Oh ! how am I going to wait until Wednesday? "

However, Jean did wait, though with great impatience, and when Wednesday dawned, she leapt out of bed to perform her tasks as soon as possible. The job ahead was long, and demanded an early start, and Jean began her lessons before breakfast so that they would be completed in time.

History and algebra were stacked away before the meal, and when it was over, geometry, arithmetic and English were attacked as vigorously. By half-past ten, such an everyday task as education was forgotten, and if a slight mistake or omission was to be found within the covers of those exercise-books . . . ' Well anyway,' she thought, ' we're not all perfect, are we? '

By eleven o'clock, the family was sitting down to a solid meal, joking merrily and planning the round-up.

" Gee ! I wish I could go with you ! " murmured Joe, as he listened to the talk.

" Do you like horses, Joe? " Jean asked eagerly.

A wistful smile crept over his face as he answered simply, " I'm just nuts on 'em ! "

" Then you'll do me ! " grinned Jean as she pushed back her chair and sprang to her feet.

Waving goodbye to those staying behind, Mr. Brownley, Bob, and Jean caught their horses and saddled them. " I don't think Diamond's ready for this work, yet," Mr. Brownley advised, as his daughter bridled the mare.

" Oh, she'll be all right, Dad, won't she? She's good at everything ; she'll do what I tell her ! " She grinned as she lifted mischievous eyes—this would be good training for the mare.

" Oh, very well, then. You'll get round me for anything, you young imp ! " her father chuckled. " But be careful. It'll be a tricky job, handling her ! "

Mrs. Brownley watched the disappearing figures with

a longing to accompany them and join in the exciting work, but her duty lay in the home, and she resigned herself to it with a little sigh.

" I hope they aren't far from the valley," said Bob as they crossed the creek not far from Ghost Cavern. " I don't think they will be," was his father's reply, " Charger knows it's time to come down, and he's possibly waiting for us."

This proved to be right, for the huge, powerful stallion was standing erect on a group of rocks, his keen senses strained for sight, sound, or smell of the man he trusted. Halting their steeds some distance to the left of the nervous mares, the riders looked on in silent admiration for a moment, before Mr. Brownley shouted, " All right, Charger, take 'em in ! "

The great head lowered and the shining body wheeled as Charger, with amazing speed and skill, fathered his mares into a small bunch and led the way through gullies and over hills towards the home paddocks.

Following at a steady pace, the three inspected the horses as closely as was possible. The brumby mares acknowledged their new leader, and his very presence seemed to calm their fears of man.

The herd thundered down a steep slope and along a narrow valley, emerging at last into the less rugged country that led up to the paddocks. Bob and Jean flanked the mares to prevent their turning aside, while their father, bringing up the rear, kept a watchful eye on all the band.

Presently the pace slackened into a slow canter, far easier for all concerned, and as there was no hurry Mr. Brownley gave them all the time they wanted. After some hard riding, the creek was reached. Charger, not deigning to notice the wooden bridge, jumped neatly to the opposite bank, with the mares following suit.

Diamond took it in her peerless style, as usual giving the impression that she enjoyed jumping to the full. The mare had behaved extremely well, considering that not long previously she had been far wilder than those mares.

' Possibly,' Jean thought, ' she recognizes her old cronies, and feels quite at home.'

At the open gates, the brumbies gave some trouble. But Charger handled them with expert precision, for whenever they hesitated, he would wheel around and nip their haunches until they were forced to make their entrance. Then, with the same amazing speed, he would push his way to the front, and lead them to the next gate. Aided by the three riders, this task was completed without very much difficulty, and eventually the band was driven into the last paddock, stocked with fresh green grass, and food and water troughs. Most of the mares, accustomed to this event, wasted no time in satisfying their wants, and the brumbies, after regarding them with a little suspicion, followed their example.

" Charger, come here ! " Mr. Brownley's commanding voice reached the pointed, sharply-pricked ears, and the stallion, who was watching his band and listening for his master, approached slowly.

" Good boy ! " praised the man as he stroked the immensely thick neck, " you've done your job well, Charger ! " The proud head lifted as intelligent eyes looked deeply into those of the man, and Jean murmured, " He understands you, Dad." The companionship between Mr. Brownley and the ' co-manager ' of the station was something of which the former felt justly proud.

Mrs. Brownley had wheeled Joe's couch on to the back verandah, from which the patient could see, at a distance, the herd of horses in the paddock ; and now, followed by the youngsters, she approached her husband. Together, they inspected the mares, foals, and yearlings clustering around the feed boxes, biting and kicking as they fought for a mouthful of corn.

" Fine lot of foals this year," remarked Mrs. Brownley happily, " but it looks as if Ginger's done for. Don't you think we'd better keep her in next winter."

" Yes, if she lasts that long," her husband replied, " in fact, we'd better keep her in through summer, too."

The family and the men discussed the good and bad points of the herd. " We'll let them settle down a bit, and separate the yearlings tomorrow," Mr. Brownley said to his wife, and Jean's eyes shone in anticipation of the hard work ahead.

It was fascinating to watch the antics of the foals as they frisked and gambolled, and when hungry ran to their dams with unerring instinct. " They've all foaled now," Bob observed, " those four must have foaled since Friday."

The sun was just beginning to lose its heat, and Mrs. Brownley hurried back to the bungalow to prepare tea. " Well, Joe," she remarked cheerily, " we've deserted you, haven't we? "

" Oh, don't worry about me, missus," was the reply, " I can see the horses pretty well from here."

Every day Joe was becoming more and more friendly, for it was almost impossible for him to be otherwise in these surroundings.

The days had passed, and still no ' preaching ' had come Joe's way; instead he had begun to realize that these people were not as many others. They had something that was so fine, so strong, lovable and appealing—something that called for the best in him. " Best in him? " Had he any " best " left? Oh, if only he had met folk like this when he was young ! He might have become like them . . . and now, it was too late : he had chosen a different road. They seemed to have no conscience to torment them like he had. They held a secret appeal for Joe, and yet there was something that kept him apart.

He was growing very fond of the youngsters. Now that he was able to sit in a chair on the verandah, he could watch and laugh at their antics, join in their plans, and listen to their stories—of the frog that went to Sunday School, of the midnight feast, of the glass that caused the fire. No one would think that they were from a ' religious ' family : they *enjoyed* life, played pranks, and yet they had told him quite freely that they were Christians.

He'd miss Jean, too. She was such a sport, a real outdoor

girl, and great with the horses, wild or tame ; yet he had heard her speak of praying as if it was quite the natural thing to do—she spoke of God as if He were one of the family. It puzzled Joe a bit, but he was growing to like it.

Yes, and he'd miss Bob. Bob would be a pal he could trust. Bob had muscle, Bob had spine, yet Bob was as tender as a nurse when it came to dressing his wound. He knew what he was doing, too . . . clever chap, that. Bob hadn't ' preached ' at all, yet Joe was conscious of something in Bob that made him uneasy when he thought back to his past life. What was it?

It was in Mr. Brownley, too. Stout-hearted, honest, jolly—and how he loved his wife ! The way he read the Bible made it out of place to call him a ' Bible-puncher '. As he read it, he seemed to fondle it as if he loved it, and when he prayed, he didn't have a book to read out of, but seemed to talk to Someone close at hand.

Yes, Joe would miss all this. He had no memory of his mother, but if he had been able to choose one, he'd have chosen one like Mrs. Brownley. She hadn't ' preached ' either, but she had made him think of a life beyond this one, and a place where he would meet God—if there was a God ; but if there wasn't a God, how could these folk live as they did? There must be a God—they *knew* Him. Oh, if only he knew Him, too !

Thoughts like these ran through Joe's mind. Ever since he had entered the Brownleys' home, discontented and longing, uncertainty and desire had followed each other in quick succession. Family prayers were no longer distasteful to Joe—he rather enjoyed them, although there was so much he didn't understand. But one conclusion stood out sharply—there must be something in Christianity, since it had made the Brownleys what they were, and already his own outlook was greatly changed.

Next morning was booked for the horses. The three students had been working hard at their lessons, so Mr. Brownley had granted them a holiday as a reward.

" Really," Mrs. Brownley laughed at breakfast, " I don't

know why you forsake an easy, sitting-down job for a hot, strenuous one ! "

" Very well, Mother," replied Jean, " I see your point. We shall do our study as usual, shan't we, kids? " A wave of alarm flowed through the youngsters, only to be dispelled by wholehearted laughter.

" And remember," cautioned Mr. Brownley, as they pushed back their chairs, " you must take it very gently, Jean. You're a young lady, you know ! "

" But I'm not ! " Jean objected, and the family roared as they vainly tried to imagine their tomboy taking it " very gently " !

" The only thing you'll ever take gently," chuckled Bob, " is a new-born foal ! "

" Shall I help you wash up, Mum? " Jean asked with forced willingness. " Mum " surveyed her with twinkling eyes. " No, I don't want you here ! You'd only break all the plates ! Go on, away with you ! " Jean gave her a bear-hug before she fled through the kitchen door.

Mr. Brownley marshalled his crew and gave orders, and then the workers, mounted on good steeds (Jean had again persuaded her father to let her ride Black Diamond), took up their positions, ready for action. " Right ! " shouted the ' Boss ', and Bob and Jean, controlling their horses well, wheeled and turned, urged and restrained, until the frightened band was clustered together around the gate which led into an adjoining paddock.

" Open the gate ! " Mr. Brownley shouted, and the youngsters complied. Instantly, Bob and Jean planted themselves in front of the opening, barring all but the yearlings from entering. It required much skill and patience to sort out the nervous colts.

" Drive some of the mares away ! " commanded Mr. Brownley as he spurred his steed, and he and Ron Smith succeeded in sending some mares and two colts to the far end of the paddock. After some more hard work the two wayward colts were brought back and ushered into the smaller paddock. Eventually the last young horse was safely on the right side of the fence. Margaret closed the gate on the milling colts, and the workers, hot and dusty, surveyed the results of their efforts.

Food and water were stored in the small paddock when the turmoil had ceased, and there was now time to rest from their exertions.

" We must brand the foals soon," remarked Mr. Brownley. " Oh, my ! We'll never get through it all by February ! " Jean's heart missed a beat. The sales were in February ; there was not much time—only four months ! It would pass quickly, Jean knew ; all too quickly. " We'll brand them tomorrow," her father continued, " and then let 'em go again. I s'pose we'll have to do it in the afternoon, so Jean can help. Oh, dear, this daughter of mine ! " He gave a wink that included all present, and then they dispersed to their various tasks.

That evening, after tea, Mr. Brownley and Joe were seated on the verandah alone. The Brownleys had prayed a great deal for Joe. He felt led now to open his heart to this man who had a secret power he wanted to possess. So they talked together of the things of God.

Mr. Brownley, who had known the ways of the world and its power, spoke of God's wonderful mercy in saving him from all that past sin.

" Can He save me like that? " asked Joe.

" Yes, of course He can."

" Wait a minute, Boss. Do you know what I was after when your kiddie shot me? I was after your horses. I'm a thief ; always have been—a liar, a drunkard when I can get the drink. Can God save a rotter like me? "

" Joe, old man, He saves to the uttermost. He Who reached down to me will reach down to you. It's for you to say if you need His help."

Joe's head was in his hands. " Oh, I will, I will ! " he cried, " God, be merciful to a sinner like me ! "

Mrs. Brownley had heard some of the conversation, and had kept the others away. There, on the verandah, the two men met with God, and Joe discovered that the secret of the Brownley household could be his, too.   A new life commenced for him that night.   Mr. Brownley's heart was humbled as he realized that God had condescended to use his home as a means of bringing salvation to this one for whom Christ had died.   Before they retired for the night, the family (minus the youngsters, who were already in bed) and Joe knelt in prayer, thanking and praising Him for the answer to many prayers, and asking for wisdom, strength, and guidance for the feet of this one so young in the faith.

9

THE sun arose to disperse a veil of mist, and a glorious day was in store. After breakfast, Mr. Brownley, followed closely by his four children, made his way to the paddocks with a light heart, for spring had dispelled all memory of winter. Everywhere there was evidence of a new awakening to life, for the trees were adorned in beautiful lacy gowns of blossom—red, pink, and white.

The foals were as frisky as ever, and needed expert handling, but at length they were in a small enclosure which also joined the main paddock, where their dams were watching with anxious eyes.

In his heart of hearts, Mr. Brownley hated this job, for he loved animals passionately, and the mere thought of hurting them made him inwardly wince. But the job had to be done, so he just made the best of it as one by one the foals were roped and branded with the hot, B-shaped branding iron.

At long last the task was completed, and Jean opened the gate into the large paddock. The young horses, with expressions of pain, anger, and bewilderment, fled towards the mares who smelt them affectionately and licked their painful rumps.

Mr. Brownley did not like Jean and the youngsters seeing this sight, but after all they had to learn for it might be their job some day. Now he said, " Jean, you and the children had better go back to your study now, and see if you can finish it by dinner-time."

So the three ran off and concentrated all their energies on what seemed, after the branding, the dullest, most uninteresting lessons that had yet been their irksome lot to study. Eventually, by means of sweating brow and fagging brain, the gruesome work was put away just before the clanging of the dinner bell sent the students rushing to the kitchen.

" What are you going to do this afternoon? " Mrs. Brownley asked as her husband dived his spoon into a pile of fruit and cream.

" Well, we've checked the horses and we're going to let them out now. We'll have to separate Ginger first, and that'll be rather tricky, as the old lady still treasures that temper of hers."

Jean's face lit up at the promise of more hard work. " And if there's time," her father added, " we'll start breaking the yearlings in." Jean gave a whoop of joy as she folded her serviette and started to clear the table hastily.

" I'll wash up, Jean," Mrs. Brownley interposed, " your services are required elsewhere ! "

" Oh, Mummy darling, thank you ever so much ! " her delighted daughter cried as she disappeared in the direction of the horse paddock.

" We'll have to get Ginger into the chute," said Mr. Brownley when the paddock was gained. " Margaret, climb up on the fence and drop the chute gate as soon as she goes through. And Frank, make sure all the other chute gates are shut: they look as if they are, but they mightn't be bolted properly. And then climb up on the fence and drop the gate when Ginger goes into the paddock. Margaret, shoo her on when you've shut the gate. Jean and Bob, help me separate Ginger from the mob."

So, mounted on quick, skilled horses, the Boss, with his two elder children, scattered the mares until Ginger and her foal became separated from her companions. Understanding each other's movements perfectly, the riders closed in on the chestnut and headed her towards the chute.

But with all her age, the mare had not lost her cunning, and as she saw the gateway drawing close, and the watchful, exultant face of Margaret, waiting in readiness to cut off her retreat, Ginger wheeled sharply, and, dodging right under Black Diamond's nose, galloped back to the herd.

As a lightning flash, the riders turned and pounded up to the far end of the paddock, overtaking the mare and foal on their way, and bringing them back to the chute. This time, Ginger, quick to tire, gave less trouble, but as she faced the chute once more she halted suddenly with only her head through the gate.

" Go on, Ginger," urged the three behind her, and Mr. Brownley flicked her rump with his whip. This proved fatal, however, for the startled mare reared suddenly at the blow, knocking Margaret's hands as she did so, and loosening the girl's hold on the gate.

Crash ! The heavy bar had fallen, and with an agonized scream, the old horse dropped, lifeless, to the ground.

Dismounting quickly, Bob and Jean lifted the gate while their father bent down to examine the body. A deathly silence reigned as he said quietly, " Broken her back ! "

The tiny filly, puzzled and frightened, sniffed anxiously at the carcass that had once satisfied all her needs and now could do so no more, and whinnied piteously. Jean's lip quivered and she turned her head—to see her little sister surreptitiously dabbing her eyes.

The hands gathered round and examined the bleeding gash in the back and right flank, and over all pervaded the same stillness—the quietness that could almost be felt.

Mrs. Brownley, hearing the crash and the ghastly scream, came running to investigate. She entered the paddock with a gasp, and this aroused her husband once more, for he said, " Oh, well, I guess it's time she went."

" Shall I bring the cart, Boss? " Clive Richardson asked, and at Mr. Brownley's nod he brought an old cart on to which Ginger was loaded, and laid to rest in one of the many hillside caves which was reserved as the animals' burial ground.

" May I look after the filly? " asked Jean, and permission was granted. After a little persuasion, the little cream foal allowed Jean to lead her to the stable where she was fed from a bottle of warm milk and made comfortable in the hay.

" Poor little thing ! " the girl sympathized, and then thought, " I'll bring Diamond in to keep her company." Running back to the paddock, she untied the mare's bridle and led her to the stable. Black Diamond was distrustful at first, but soon followed her mistress inside, where she was fed with some oats.

Jean left them making friendly overtures to each other, and wended her way back to where the family was discussing the accident. " Poor old Ginger," murmured Mr. Brownley, " she was the first mare I bought." For though Ginger's temper was renowned, the man had been very fond of her. There was a pause before his wife concluded, " Oh, well, it's no good moping. Better get on with the work."

The workers dispersed, and Mrs. Brownley, returning to the house, exclaimed, " Oh, Joe ! I'd forgotten all about you ! I'm terribly sorry ! "

" Oh, that's quite all right, missus," was the response, " what . . . happened? "

Mrs. Brownley's face clouded again. " They were trying to get Ginger in the chute, and she reared and hit Margaret's hands, and made her drop the gate . . . right on to the mare's back. They've just put her body in the burial cave."

" Oh ! Missus ! I'm awfully sorry ! " was all Joe said—there was nothing more to say.

" Ginger . . . was my husband's first mare. He was pretty fond of her. Oh, well, no use crying over spilt milk. But it's hard lines on the foal ! "

" Yes, poor little thing ! She must be lonely ! " And Joe sighed wistfully.

Tea was a quiet meal that day. Mr. Brownley had opened all the gates, and Charger had piloted his mares to their mountain home. Jean had kept vigil on Creamy, as she named the filly, and already Black Diamond and she were fast friends. The little lonely foal had found companionship in the black mare. The evening was spent quietly, too, and the family retired early to bed.

But next morning the usual high spirits were practically restored, and work went on as usual. Joe was able to do odd jobs, such as wiping up and preparing the vegetables, and he did them all with the greatest willingness, hoping to repay in some measure the debt that he felt he owed the Brownleys.

Doctor Rex had visited him a few times, and had pronounced steady progress. The days passed quickly for the convalescent, and one day, the doctor proclaimed him to be ' A.1 '. Joe donned his clothes—now clean and mended —for the first time for months, and walked gingerly around the kitchen on shaky legs. His feelings were mixed, for, glad as he was to be active once more, he hated the thought of leaving this household that had come to mean so much to him—above all, where he had passed from death unto life.

" Well, Joe, what now? " asked Mr. Brownley, " got any plans? "

" No, Boss, but I feel I'd like to work for you with no pay so as to repay you all for what you've been to me."

" Oh, nonsense, Joe. It was *He* Who restored, not us.

But thinking it over, I could very well do with another hand to help with all those brumbies. We're training them for the sales, and for the show. The missus and I hope to help Bob to train for a doctor with the cash they'll make. What about your coming in on the job, too? "

"Shake hands on it, Boss. I'll never go back on you, never."

"Whoa back! Whoa! Steady there!" The breaking-in of the yearlings was in full swing, and Jean was trying out a bay who had a deep-rooted objection to the saddle. "This one will be a good goer when he's tamed," she remarked, "he has plenty of fight in him."

"Like a change?" her father offered, but if there was anything Jean hated it was defeat, so she shook her head grimly as the bay shot skywards and landed on stiff fore-feet.

Most of the horses were coaxed and broken-in gently, but no amount of coaxing was profitable to the bad-tempered ones.

"That's Ginger's colt, isn't it?" asked Bob. "No wonder he has hot blood!" But at long last the bay was beaten. Wearily he ceased to buck, acknowledging the conquest of discipline.

Jean cantered him once around the paddock and dismounted, a little shaken, but gleeful at her success. The girl ' liked it rough ', and had even been disappointed when a horse gave no trouble.

"Look at those clouds," remarked Frank, "I guess there'll be a storm soon!" The atmosphere was stifling, and the workers literally dripped. "Yes, I think so, too," Bob put in, "it's getting steamy now."

Clang! clang! "There's the bell! Race you all in to tea!" challenged Jean. The horses were hastily turned loose, and equipment was stored in the stable, before the hungry people thronged the kitchen. "Gee! I'm boiling!" Margaret exclaimed, "I feel as if I can't breathe. Isn't the air close?"

The family sat down to a cool, refreshing salad, which revived them considerably. "That colt of Ginger's is the worst-tempered horse I've ever met!" Mr. Brownley remarked, "I don't think any of her other colts have been quite as bad. But he's coming to realize that he's not boss, I think."

"Who's been handling him?" his wife asked immediately.

"Who do you think, dear?" Jean studied her plate modestly.

"I suppose it was our 'wild-woman', as usual, eh, Jean?" The girl looked up and two small dimples appeared in her cheeks.

"You know, we really shouldn't let you ride all the worst horses, Jean. You're only a girl, after all!"

"Yes, but what a girl!" chuckled Bob, for he admired his sister's skill and pluck.

"It's a good thing for you that you were made for the saddle," Mr. Brownley continued, "or I'd be more stern!"

Jean glowed at this praise, for to hear this from her father was even better than to be called a tomboy.

"Oh, well," she said happily, "I haven't been bitten or kicked yet, and I've never been hurt when I was bucked."

"All the same, you must always be careful, for I'd hate to have you hobbling around on crutches!"

Crash! Thunder followed a flicker of lightning, as the threatened storm broke suddenly. Even Mr. Brownley glanced up quickly to see the hills and valleys illuminated with a purple sheet of light. After only two seconds, the house was shaken as a deep, gathering roar broke the stillness, and then the heavens were rent by vivid forked lightning that exploded almost over the house with an ear-splitting crack.

"I wish it would rain," muttered Mr. Brownley, but his words were drowned in a deafening boom.

" It's coming nearer," his wife answered, " I hope the horses are all right." At the word " horses ", an awful thought flashed across Jean's brain. Creamy was out in the paddock ! She would be frightened to death, and cold. She was rather delicate, and could easily become ill.

" I must get her," thought the girl ; " just like me to be so careless ! "

She excused herself and slipped away, not daring to tell of her mission, in case the others prevented her going. Donning mac, gum-boots and sou'wester, she climbed out of the window and tip-toed off the verandah.

As she stepped into the vegetable patch, a drop of water caught her nose, and another the brim of her sou'wester. The rain had started, and steadily increased in weight and force. A wind rose rapidly and drove the rain hard against her face.   The lightning flashed around the girl and thunder echoed and re-echoed among the mountains.

Pushing her way against the howling gale, Jean plodded gamely on and was soon engulfed in the darkness. She produced her torch to light her way. In an instant, the ground was soaked, and she had to splash through puddles to reach her objective.

Crash ! A blazing fork of fire shot upwards, met another, and exploded with a sound like that of a rifle-shot, and the thunder, following closely, resembled a cannon's boom. It was really a wonderful sight to see the mountains sil-houetted against a purple sky at every flash of lightning, and the raindrops that glittered like giant jewels, but Jean had neither time nor inclination to appreciate the wonder of it.

Crash ! Another flash of lightning, and a huge gum hit the ground with force, its foliage burning fiercely as the impact sent up a shower of sparks. However, the wind and rain extinguished that danger quickly, and Jean thanked God for the escape.

After what seemed an age, she reached the horse pad-dock and opened the gate. There, cowering beside Black Diamond, the small cream foal was trembling in every limb. Diamond whinnied a welcome as Jean approached and said, " Come on, Creamy, come along, girlie." She produced a lead rope and slipped it over Creamy's head. The filly, almost paralyzed with fear, hadn't the strength to struggle, and allowed herself to be led away after Jean had given Diamond a word and a pat.

" Come on, Creamy," urged the girl, closing the gate, " we must hurry now." Another clap of thunder pealed its warning across the heavens, and the foal shivered. Jean flung her arm around the filly's neck and coaxed desperately. She tugged hard at the rope, and proceeded as quickly as was possible.

They skirted a thickly-wooded slope, and wended their way through a narrow passage of rocks before emerging into flat, open fields once more. " Come on, Creamy," the girl encouraged, for the pace was slackening, " we haven't far to go now."

Slowly but surely, the two approached the stable. A pink glow lit up the sky as Jean glanced at the house, and thus enabled her to pick out two figures on the verandah. They had seen her, too, for now they came running towards her with torches, and proved to be Mr. Brownley and Bob.

When Creamy was safely installed on a bed of hay, and Jean had warmed the glistening, quivering body, Mr. Brownley said, " You shouldn't have done it, Jean. You could have been struck ! "

" Creamy could have been, too, and she's so delicate."

" Isn't your life worth more than a horse's? " asked her father. Jean said nothing, but followed him inside to get some warm milk for the filly.

IO

"HEIGH-HO!" Jean yawned as she stretched luxuriously beneath the bed-clothes. She started to sing, " It's nice to get up in the morning, but it's nicer to stay in bed! " Then, after a pause, she added, " No, it isn't! I hate lying in bed in the morning—I'd rather be up in the cold, cold air! "

Her noise woke Margaret, sleeping close by, who murmured drowsily and opened her eyes. " Brrrr! " she shivered, " it's frosty this morning! "

" Come on, lazybones! " bantered her elder sister, " my child, don't you know it's *very healthy* to be up with the lark? "

" Then why aren't you? " the other retaliated.

" Because the lazy old bird isn't up himself yet! "

Jean tried to turn a somersault beneath the clothes, and succeeded in dragging them to the ground as she fell out of bed, clambering back immediately. " Oh, well, it's time I raised my portly person." She swung her legs to the ground and donned kimono and slippers. " I go, dear Margaret, to gently call thy fond brethren from their slumbers."

" Whacko! Now for it! I wouldn't be them for a fortune! " Margaret ejaculated as she lay back and listened for the ominous sounds of bumping and banging that soon issued from the neighbouring bedroom.

Shortly after breakfast, the mail arrived in the ' box-on-wheels ', as they had christened the Ford sedan. " Only one . . . for Mother," announced Bob, who had brought it in from the mail-box. Mrs. Brownley tore open the envelope and scanned the letter.

"It's from Evelyn," she remarked after a moment, naming her sister, "and she wants to know if she and Beryl could stay here for a month. Beryl's convalescing after double pneumonia, and being delicate, it's taken it out of her a lot, so the doctor recommends the mountain air. It'll be all right for them to come, won't it, dear?"

"Yes, of course," replied her husband, "there's always the barn and the cowshed!" His eyes twinkled. "You know, I think it's marvellous, the way this house extends itself with the greatest of ease. When do they want to come?"

Mrs. Brownley consulted her letter and said, "As soon as possible. Let me see . . . if I write today, the letter will get to Newcastle by Tuesday. I'll ask them to let me know when they can come."

So Mrs. Brownley sent the letter off next day, and it slipped into the Wren letter box on Tuesday, as predicted. Mrs. Wren replied that they could be there by the next Saturday, and many thanks.

Mrs. Brownley received the answer on Thursday, and at once the household threw all its energy into preparing for the visitors. Two camp beds were erected on the back verandah for the girls, as Mrs. Wren and her daughter were to share their room.

The children awaited their arrival with mixed feelings, for they had visited their aunt, uncle, and thirteen-year-old cousin over a year ago. Mr. Wren was rather quiet, though a very kind and generous man, while his wife was gentle and rather weak-charactered. Beryl had inherited these traits, and was too sedate and prim to appeal very much to the Brownley youngsters. However, they tried to see only the good qualities and overlook the rest.

Saturday dawned, and Mr. Brownley drove the old truck to the tiny side-station twenty-five miles away, returning late at night with the two visitors.

Once inside the gate he tooted the horn loudly, and the rest of the family came out of the house to greet them.

Beryl stepped down from the lorry, and Mr. Brownley assisted her mother. They were warmly embraced, and then the party went into the house where a delicious aroma of hot supper drew them. Mr. Brownley drove the truck to an old shed, and, assisted by Bob and Jean, unloaded the luggage.

" Well, how are you? " " Did you have a good journey? " " And how's Beryl? " " How's Uncle Douglas? " " How long has Beryl been ill? " Questions flew back and forth across the supper table.

Beryl surveyed her surroundings timidly, and fiddled with her handkerchief, replying to the questions addressed to her in a small, but perfectly-cultured, voice.

When the last cake was eaten, and all the news told, Mrs. Brownley suggested that the best place now was bed, so, showing the newcomers to their room, the family left them and retired for the night.

Next morning, Margaret woke early, and jumped out of bed to shake Jean. " Shall I call Beryl? " she asked as her victim roused.

" No," was the reply, " she might be tired and want to sleep in."

" But she might want to watch the milking."

" Oh well, there's plenty of time to do that ! Besides . . ." Jean grinned, " . . . I've an idea that she may object to being disturbed at this hour. Most towneys do ! "

Margaret glanced at the little clock which declared the time to be a quarter to five, and agreed softly, " Yes, perhaps so."

Some time later, Margaret and Frank followed Bob and Jean to the kitchen, their appetites aggravated by their early morning work.

" Sh-h-h ! " cautioned Mrs. Brownley, " they're still asleep. I'll take some breakfast in soon."

" They'll be late for church if they don't get up soon," her husband put in, " it's about time we called them."

So as soon as breakfast was finished, a dainty breakfast

tray was carried in to the guests. " What's the time, dear? " asked Mrs. Wren as her sister drew up a chair on which to rest the tray.

" It's half-past seven now," was Mrs. Brownley's answer, " we leave at about half-past nine."

The other gasped. " I'll never be ready in time ! I must fly ! "

" Take it easy, Evelyn, there's plenty of time if you don't hang around."

Mrs. Brownley left her sister still in a panic and declaring that she wouldn't have half enough time to do her hair. The Brownleys carried out their allotted work as quickly as possible, and then prepared for the journey, while Mrs. Wren and Beryl " flew " around their room, taking, as it seemed to the others, an infinite amount of time to adorn themselves with elaborate clothes.

As they couldn't ride, Pepper was harnessed to the buggy while the other horses were saddled and the lunch stored in readiness.

" Aren't they ready yet? " Jean wondered impatiently, and at her mother's suggestion, went to the bedroom to remind them of the time. She found Beryl laboriously brushing her long flaxen curls.

" It's half-past nine," she remarked, and the other girl exclaimed in alarm, " Oh ! I haven't done my hair yet ! "

" That'll do, won't it? It looks all right," Jean replied, eyeing with some scorn the fair tresses. " Hurry up, or we'll be late . . . say, do you like long hair? "

" Of course I do ! It makes a girl more becoming ! "

Jean's mouth opened slightly ; she shrugged her shoulders and remarked, " Well, if I had my way, I'd cut all plaits off ! "

Finally, Mrs. Wren and her daughter were safely installed in the buggy, and the rough journey downhill began. Mrs. Brownley drove as carefully as possible, but even so the passengers were rather shaken when they arrived at church.

When the service had finished, the Brownley household chatted to this one and that, introducing the newcomers and discussing scraps of news. Leisurely they all formed one big circle and unwrapped their lunches.

Mrs. Wren seated herself on the grass with obvious distaste and reluctance. " I wish I'd brought my overcoat," she sighed, " I shall get grass stains on my frock," and if she had fully known the company to which she was speaking, she would have kept her thoughts to herself. However, the others passed this by as being part of the ' towney's ' make-up.

As usual, the children finished their meal long before the adults, and, not content to sit and listen to the gossip, they wandered off in a crowd in search of entertainment more to their liking.

Bob and Jean soon tired of their elders' conversation, too, and rose to go for a walk. " Coming, Beryl? " the boy invited, but Beryl refused politely, whether because she was interested in the talk, or shy, or just unfriendly, the pair could not determine.

They went off slowly, and Jean, referring to the morning's incident, said, " I asked Beryl if she liked long hair, and she said, ' Of course I do ! It makes a girl more becoming ! ' " Bob gave a sudden shout of laughter, and Jean continued, " I can't stand that sissy, I'm sick of her already, and I don't know how I'm going to put up with her for a whole month ! "

Bob's face grew serious. " You know, Jean, you're awfully intolerant. She possibly hates you, too. I mean, she's probably awfully lonely and shy, and wishes we weren't so rough. You ought to remember we are far from perfect, ourselves."

" Yes, but she's unbearable ! "

" Well, I suppose it's her parents and her upbringing. Poor kid ! Surely she can't be happy ? Anyway, I think we ought to be as friendly as possible to her, and make her feel at home. She might be all right, underneath."

"It will be frightfully hard," sighed Jean, "but I'll try!"

By this time they had reached the creek, and jumped lightly across it, pushing their way on through dense scrub and tall gums. "I think we'd better go back now," Bob advised after a while, and as they turned to retrace their steps, he remembered that he hadn't told Jean of the new desire that had taken hold of him.

'I'll tell her now,' he thought, and began, "Jean, you know when I was nursing Joe? . . . " he paused, " —well, I often used to get . . . a funny feeling. . . ." He hesitated again, and Jean linked her arm in his, to encourage him. "I felt I wanted something . . . badly . . . and I couldn't find out what it was. And then, one morning, it dawned on me!" There was a deep, desperate longing in his voice as he cried, " I want to be a medical missionary!"

Jean, who understood her brother's every action, every word, squeezed his arm in sympathy. "To save souls as well as bodies," the boy murmured.

"Bob, old chap, we'll have to pray about it really hard. I'm sure it'll turn out all right if we do. It's the same with Black Diamond. I pray about her morning and night, and somehow, I feel God will grant my wish. In any case, He won't make any mistake."

"I suppose I should have more faith," the other joined in, "but it's pretty hard!"

"Yes, I know; my faith is being tested, too."

Returning to the church, the two found the afternoon services due to begin. Jean took her position at the harmonium, noticing that Beryl was the only one who was sitting perfectly still. "Of course, *she* would!" the girl thought grimly, and then, remembering Bob's advice, she prayed, "O God, please help me to be more friendly to her!"

"Now," began Miss Paton, "choruses!" Half a dozen voices cried at once, and Miss Paton covered her ears. "One at a time, if you have that much patience," she laughed, " Johnny, what's yours? " " Jethuth lovth me," lisped the baby of the Sunday School, eagerly.

They sang it through, and many others with it, granting all the requests. But before the second chorus had come to an end, Miss Paton, Bob, and Jean had realized that Beryl's voice was something out of the ordinary. She reached the highest notes with easily rounded, mellow tones that drew attention.

" Didn't know she could sing ! " Jean thought with natural admiration, " p'r'aps she's not so bad after all . . . but I wish she wasn't so prim and proper ! "

Miss Paton spoke about Joseph's life—his dreams, his brothers' jealousy, his captivity, and finally, his crown. With more choruses the meeting closed, not long before the church service, and the gathering dispersed to the various homes.

" Would you like to watch us milk the cows? " Margaret invited Beryl as they closed the front gate. Beryl wasn't a scrap interested in milking, but she remembered what her mother had said in the train : " Now, dear, you must be friendly with the children, and join in their games, or they can't be friendly with you," so she agreed with pretended enthusiasm.

" Yes, I'd like to, thank you."

" Well, we're going down right now. You'd better change your dress, and wear some gum-boots, 'cause it's pretty muddy after the rain we had last week."

The words struck dismay into the other's heart. " Muddy ! " she thought despairingly, " it'll splash my stockings and . . . I haven't any gum-boots ! " She confessed this to Margaret who instantly replied, " I'll lend you an old pair of Jean's, and you can take your stockings off."

" But I'll get a cold after wearing them all day ! "

" Why? " Margaret overruled all objections and presented Beryl with the gum-boots.

There was no retreating now, so the girl exchanged her embroidered silk dress for a plainer, linen one. " I'd better leave my stockings on," she thought, " I hope they won't be soiled."

Margaret was waiting impatiently on the back step. " Come on, Beryl," was her greeting, " you've been ages. Here, d'you mind carrying these buckets? " She handed her two, and continued her journey, clanging her burden loudly. Beryl took the buckets gingerly, holding them at arm's length to prevent their touching her dress.

" Bob's bringing the cows in now," commented Margaret as she gazed out across the paddocks. " See? Through that big gate. He's just given them a drink at the dam. By the time he's here, we'll have everything ready. Come on . . . what's up? "

For Beryl was standing stock still, eyeing with horror and loathing a vast puddle of mud that confronted her. Margaret was mystified for a moment, until she realized the cause of the trouble. ' P'r'aps she isn't used to mud,' she thought ; then aloud she said, " Come on, it's all right with gum-boots on. It always gets like this after rain, but the sun dries it up fairly quickly." Beryl wrinkled her small nose elegantly, and skirted the broad patch of mud.

" You can't dodge it all like that ! " Margaret giggled, " it's tons worse down at the cowshed."

They proceeded on their way, meeting Jean and Frank busy with the machines. Beryl flatly refused to cross the deep mud that bore the imprints of many hooves, and she was standing some distance away, watching the others with some interest, when a stifled scream escaped her lips.

Behind her the cows had been approaching with ponderous tread, and had halted not ten yards away. Beryl took to flight, not daring to glance back until she had gained the safety of a giant gum.

The cows were not chasing her wildly, eager to gore her to pieces, as she had imagined, but instead they were placidly moving into their accustomed bails, thinking fondly of a feed of corn. Slowly Beryl advanced, noting that no one was laughing at her, but rather inviting her to watch the milking from a closer spot.

But that barrier of mud kept Beryl a good ten yards from the cowshed, and standing alone there, the girl wished heartily that she had never accepted Margaret's offer.

After some time, every cow had been loosened and turned into the neighbouring paddock, and the workers carried their buckets to the dairy. Beryl followed miserably, and pretended to take an interest in the procedure of separating the cream from the milk. Thankfully, she accompanied them to the kitchen at last, where a sumptuous spread burdened the table.

After tea, the household gathered on the verandah to capture the last warm light of the waning sun, and then, according to the habit of all country people—' early to bed, early to rise '—they retired for the night.

Next morning, the children had milked the cows and prepared for breakfast before Beryl, clad in the fourth different frock she had worn in three days, presented herself and asked shyly if she could help.

" It's all done now, dear," was Mrs. Brownley's kind reply, " is your mother ready for her breakfast? "

" She's getting up now," the girl answered, " she will be out in a short while."

Mrs. Wren appeared later, in a blue silk kimono, her hair a mass of curling pins, and her eyes half-shut with lingering sleep.

After breakfast, Mrs. Brownley suggested that Jean should do her lessons in the afternoon during her aunt's stay, so that Beryl would be entertained throughout the day.

So with some foreboding, the older girl led the younger to the horse paddock, asking, " Do you like horses, Beryl? "

" Oh, yes, they're all right," was the polite but unfeeling response. Jean shrugged her shoulders as a new feeling of dislike surged within her. She didn't understand people who were so disinterested in animals, but realized that she was really being rather selfish.

" Oh, well," she said cheerily, " I don't suppose everybody's the same. But you'll like Black Diamond. I didn't ride her yesterday because she needs a rest now and then. Pepper's a dear old thing, but he's not in the same street as Diamond—he's had his best day long ago. Oh, and Creamy! You'll love her! She's Ginger's foal—you know, Dad told you about Ginger—she's a pretty little thing, and now she's awfully friendly. If her mother had lived, the foal would have copied her and become a vicious little brute, but as she spends most of her time with Diamond, she's very gentle and sweet-natured."

By this time they had entered the horse paddock and Jean whistled Diamond, who trotted up quickly, with Creamy following by her side. At their approach, Beryl's pallor changed to a dead white, and she backed towards the gate.

"They won't hurt you," reassured Jean, noting this. "Come on, come here and pat them." But Beryl lacked the courage, and stood some yards away while the older girl fondly caressed the horses.

The mare and filly made an attractive picture as they nuzzled Jean—Black Diamond, the personification of majestic, dignified nobility, mingled with her gentle nature which had made itself evident once the coating of wildness had been worn away by love—and Creamy, delicate yet frisky, cheeky though gentle, curious at every new thing, learning new ways and habits, finding new occupations every day, and developing according to the pattern of her foster-mother.

Slowly but surely Beryl drew closer until she reached out a trembling hand and stroked the tiny white nose that wrinkled as it sought to catch some knowledge of this stranger. Beryl, strangely fascinated, reached further, and stroked the filly's neck.

Up to this time, animals had not interested her, but this dear little baby thing won her affection completely. She grew less fearful, and laughed delightedly when Creamy stuck her nose in the girl's chest. Jean was surprised, but merely commented, " She's friendly, isn't she? "

After a while, Beryl waxed bold and stroked Diamond's

neck, realizing how beautiful the mare was, and how gentle ; and also how silly she, Beryl, had been for being frightened of the horses.

It was almost with regret that she followed Jean back through the gate. " Creamy is so sweet, and I like her," she said a little shyly.

" Yes, I think so," responded the other, " and do you like Black Diamond? " When Beryl had answered that she did, Jean continued, " I say, Beryl, would you like to learn how to ride? "

Beryl hesitated. An hour ago, she would have refused, but now she faltered, " Well, I'd like to ride Creamy ! "

Jean controlled her mirth with difficulty, and replied, " You'll be able to if you come again *next year*—that is, if she's been broken in properly by then. But now she'd either sink under your weight, or buck you off ! "

This silenced Beryl for a few minutes, and Jean added, " But would you really like to ride? "

Again the younger girl hesitated, and finally she said, " Yes, I think I would—but not on those big horses. I might fall off ! "

" Oh, you wouldn't ! " Jean countered, " you know, all this bosh about falling off is only a crazy idea that inexperienced people have. You don't know how simple it is : you just park yourself in the saddle, and take hold of the reins and the stirrups, and then . . . well, the horse just goes, and you go, too. I met a man at the last Sydney Show who owns a riding school in Sydney, and he said that the very first lesson he teaches new riders how to get on and off, how to hold the reins and use the stirrups, and then he takes them out for a ride—walking, trotting, and cantering. The hardest part is learning to control the horse, and the rest is only a matter of practice. Well, would you like to try? Or aren't you game? "

Beryl met the challenge well. She was finding that she, too, wanted to excel like her brilliant cousins, so now she accepted bravely.

"All right," Jean agreed, "like to start now?"

Beryl looked at her steadily : she had taken the first step, and now she could not look back. "Yes," she responded briefly, "right now!" She did not realize until weeks later, that Creamy had been the turning point of her whole outlook on life.

II

JEAN and Beryl hurried to the house, where Beryl put on an old pair of trousers that had done Jean yeoman service, and then went back to the horse paddock via the stable.

"There's an old grey here—as gentle as a lamb—he'll be just right for you," said Jean as she opened the gate. "There he is, over in the far corner. He's quite easy to catch. Come on, never mind all these other horses; they won't hurt you. They're all the saddle horses that the family and the men use—good stockhorses, too."

They threaded their way through more than a dozen horses of various colours, and advanced towards an old grey pony who was sleepily rubbing his head against the fence. "Here, Timmy," Jean coaxed as she slipped the bridle over his head. Timmy looked at her in mild surprise and snorted a little reproachfully, but offered no resistance.

Turning to Beryl, Jean remarked, "It's a good thing to be able to saddle your horse first. It's quite easy, if you watch carefully. And if you make friends with him before you ride, you'll find he'll understand you better, and you'll enjoy yourself more."

Beryl was an apt pupil and took the advice sensibly. She went to Timmy's head and slowly stroked his neck. "He can stand a lot of that," laughed Jean, " you can almost hear him purring ! "

She had noticed the sudden change in Beryl, dating from the time she had first seen Creamy, and she had begun to admire the girl who, to her mind, was ' showing more sense '. Beryl indeed seemed to have forgotten her fear of animals, though inwardly she quaked and reproved herself for so foolishly accepting the challenge.

Jean buckled the girth and said, " Now we're ready. I'll show you how to mount first. You face the tail—like this—and then you take the reins in your left hand—hold them like this : then you put this foot in the stirrup, and hang on to the pommel with your left hand, the back of the saddle with your right hand, and you get up and swing your other leg over, like this ! "

She swung agilely into the saddle, and continued, " Now you hold the reins like this, in your left hand, and when you want to turn, you pull him round like this." She demonstrated, adding, " Oh, and of course, you must always catch them and mount on the near side—that's the left side —and never on the off. That's very important, because any but a slug—a quiet horse—will kick up a shindy if you don't."

Jean showed how to dismount, and said, " Now you try ! "

" Will he go if I get on? " Beryl quavered. Jean restrained a laugh, replying, " Oh, no ! It takes more than that to make Timmy go ! " Beryl clambered awkwardly into the saddle, assisted by the older girl who wrinkled her nose rather impatiently at this display of clumsiness.

Once mounted, the pupil felt more confident, and clasped the reins according to instructions. Jean shortened the stirrups a little, and finally said, " Well, you're all set now. I'll saddle Diamond and we'll go for a ride." She showed Beryl how to control the horse, and ran off to catch the black mare, calling back as she ran, " Bring Timmy up here ! "

Beryl flicked the reins nervously, and the grey moved off slowly. The girl gripped the pommel hard, striving to keep her unpractised balance, but by the time she had reached the fence, she was becoming accustomed to the gait of the horse, and very gradually released her hold.

Jean trotted up on Diamond, and together they made their way across smooth paddocks that offered good riding. Presently, they came to the foot of a slope, and Jean quickened Diamond's pace from a walk to a canter.

" Shorten the reins," she called back, " and kick hard ! "

Beryl flapped her legs uselessly against Timmy's flanks, so Jean wheeled Diamond and brought her alongside, flicking the gelding's rump. Timmy started forward, a look of pained surprise on his face, and Beryl, after letting out a shriek, found the loping stride easy and thrilling.

At the top of the rise, Timmy slowed to a jog. Beryl bumped and jolted all over the saddle, and nearly fell off. She instinctively grasped the pommel, her teeth clenched, and Jean said, " Rise in the stirrups. Look, like this . . ." she demonstrated, but Beryl was too shaken to make any effort on her part.

She managed to pull Timmy up to a walk, and, deathly white, implored Jean to let her get off. The older girl explained how to trot in comfort, remarking as Beryl still bumped and bounced that it only needed practice.

Eventually they returned to the horse paddock, and Beryl mounted and dismounted several times before Jean was satisfied.

Feeling stiff but triumphant, she followed her cousin to the homestead, where she changed in good time for dinner. Jean could not find reason for preferring dresses to jodhpurs, but she kept her feelings secret.

After the meal, she began her lessons, but all the time she could not help thinking of the morning's incident, and how it had affected her " prim and proper " cousin.

" Boundary ! That's six for us, and good for you, Beryl ! "

looked up in amazement . . . the faultless, colourful playing was something she had never heard before.

The girl rose and crept to the lounge door, to find the youngsters gazing through the French window, full of admiration. Beryl, unaware of their presence, went on playing to the end.

Her audience, which had been increased by Mrs. Brownley, gasped with delight, and Beryl swung round sharply, colouring a little as she saw that she was the centre of attraction. Mrs. Wren had entered, and was smiling at her daughter.

" Didn't know you could play," was Jean's tribute, " why didn't you tell us before? "

" That was lovely, dear," Mrs. Brownley broke in, " play some more." Beryl, somewhat overwhelmed by all this attention, complied with a skilful rendering of the Intermezzo from *Cavalleria Rusticana*.

" Why didn't you play before? " asked Jean when the last chords had died away.

" Well, there didn't seem to be an opportunity . . ."

" And also," Mrs. Wren finished, " I think Beryl was shy."

" Gee ! You're not bad, anyway," Frank praised, and Margaret added, " How long have you been learning? "

" Three years," was the response, and Mrs. Brownley said to herself, " The child is certainly talented."

They left Beryl in peace, and returned to their duties, listening entranced as the pianist played piece after piece, transforming the old, untuned piano into an instrument of sweet harmony.

The dinner bell rang at last, and Jean, who had more than once forsaken her studies to listen to the music, thankfully stored her books in her desk and went to the bathroom to wash her hands.

During dinner the incident of the morning was discussed, and Beryl's talent was praised until the girl in question felt successive hot and cold waves in her cheeks.

" Well, tonight, Beryl, I shall ask you to do your stuff,

while we sit and let the sounds of music creep in our ears."

"Yes, Uncle Shakespeare," Beryl laughed happily as she bit into her second apple.

"We'd better be getting ready soon." Bob arose and pulled out his mother's chair.

"I'll have to change," Beryl called as she vanished into the bedroom, "I shan't be long." She reappeared after some moments, looking smart in neat grey jodhpurs which had been sent from Newcastle, with her hair tied in two plaits.

The younger Brownleys raced outside after her, each catching and saddling his own horse.

"That's too loose, isn't it, Jean?" asked Beryl as she buckled Pepper's girth.

"Yes, put it one hole further," advised the other, secretly admiring her cousin's deftness.

The three adults waved goodbye from the verandah, and the party cantered slowly towards the gate. Approaching it, the Brownleys quickened the pace and jumped the wide gate together.

Beryl watched them wistfully as she bent down to open the gate for herself, and Bob, turning back, laughed, "That was unrehearsed! I say, Beryl, would you like to learn to jump?"

Beryl's riding had improved so rapidly that this was not an impossible suggestion. Her heart beat fast as she answered, "Yes, I'd love to!"

"She's game!" murmured Jean, who had drawn rein beside her brother.

"Well," Bob continued, "there's a hollow not far from here which some men have been clearing, and there are plenty of logs there that you could try."

"It's quite easy," put in Frank who had joined the group with Margaret, "it feels a bit funny at first, but you soon get used to that."

The horses trotted down the mountain side, Beryl sitting more or less comfortably in the saddle.

After half-an-hour's riding, they emerged into a log-strewn even patch of ground, two hundred yards square, ideal for jumping. The fallen trees ranged in thickness from saplings to giant gums—excellent for a beginner.

" We'll roll these out of the way," said Bob, dismounting from Rover and attaching his reins to a shrub, " and leave the best ones with good spaces between each."

They worked energetically, until a jumping field was prepared. " Now, Beryl," Bob instructed, " there's nothing to it. You just sit tight and lift your horse over the top."

He showed her how it was done, and Beryl, inwardly nervous, approached the first small log at a canter. Pepper, well practised with trainees, took it gently, and Beryl, apart from being thrown on to his neck when he landed, managed to keep her seat quite well.

" How is it? " asked Jean when she had pulled up.

" Not bad." The reply was doubtful. Bob laughed, " It's easy, isn't it? You'll like it better the more you do it. Now try again."

Beryl returned to the hurdle, and this time found it easier and more enjoyable. They kept her practising until she could do it correctly, and then she went over the larger logs, losing her nervousness and feeling more thrilled at each jump.

" That's fine ! " Bob applauded, " you're going to be a great horsewoman if you keep it up ! " And then he realized dully that she couldn't keep it up, for she did not possess a horse.

' It's a shame,' he thought, ' she could be jolly good at riding.'

The others joined her and the five went through the course together. Then they decided not to spend any more time there, so they turned their horses' heads, and made their way along an overgrown track in a westerly direction towards Aroonta Valley.

" How far is the valley from here? " asked Beryl, when they had cantered some distance.

" Oh, only about three more miles now," Jean answered.

Only three more miles ! It was not far to the saddle-hardened Brownleys, but it made Beryl almost wish she had not come. Three weeks of riding does not take away all stiffness, but the girl put a brave face on the matter, and joked gaily as they journeyed west.

" Isn't it hot ! " sighed Jean, " it's more like summer than spring. Look, Diamond is sweating like anything ! "

" Better take it easy," Bob advised, " we can have a drink at the water-hole in the valley if the horses aren't too steamy. We're nearly there now."

His words proved to be true, for shortly after this speech, the party topped a low rise and gazed down at a panorama of rich green grass and blue shimmering water that reflected the surrounding trees with mirror-like clarity.

" Oh ! " gasped Beryl, " isn't it beautiful ! "

They wended their way downwards through dense scrub, halting by the water-hole for a cherished drink.

" Who wants their tucker now? " Bob asked needlessly, extracting cake and fruit from his saddle-pouch. The company arranged themselves under a leafy gum and devoured their ' afternoon tea ' hungrily, topping it with small bars of home-made chocolate.

" It's time we returned to ' le château '," Bob said at last, jumping up. They commenced their homeward journey, and the sun had lost its heat by the time they reached the gate.

After tea, the household gathered in the lounge and coaxed Beryl into playing again. Retiring and shy, the girl was not used to airing her talent, but she soon felt at home and played her best. Mr. Brownley and Bob, who had not heard her before, sat almost spellbound as the entrancing music drifted through the room.

At last, she finished the Moonlight Sonata, and after the applause Jean said, " Beryl can sing, too ! "

" How did you know? " the girl asked in surprised innocence, and then, realizing that she had fallen into a trap, she hastened to make amends with, " I mean, of course I can't ! "

Jean raised one eyebrow. " Then why do you sing so beautifully at Sunday School? "

" I don't ! I only make an awful row ! "

" Quit the modesty ! " Bob cut in, " Mother, wouldn't you like to hear Beryl sing? "

" I'd love to ! " exclaimed Mrs. Brownley, " do sing us something, dear."

Beryl saw that there was no way of dodging it, so she said lamely, " Well, what shall I sing? "

" Do you know ' The Bells of St. Mary's '? "

" Yes."

" Well, here it is ! " Jean opened the song at the first page, and placed it in front of her cousin.

Beryl sang the verse with low, mellow tones and went on with the chorus, reaching the highest notes in a full clear voice that showed proof that she was gifted. The audience sat in silence until the song had ended.

A burst of applause followed the item, broken by exclamations of surprise and delight. Beryl was asked to play and sing as much as she liked all the next week, so that the family would be entertained.

" She hasn't turned out bad, has she? " Bob remarked as he and Jean were departing to their bedrooms.

" No . . . I didn't think she had all that up her sleeve ; she looked pretty green when she first came, but she's proved that she's got fine stuff in her."

During the past weeks, Jean's intolerance had worn away, replaced by a wholesome respect of other viewpoints than her own, and her parents, noting this, were pleasantly surprised.

The remaining days passed quickly, until it was the day of the visitors' departure. During the last days, there had been some rather mysterious consultations, letters sent, and arrangements made with the railways.

Beryl was not at all keen to go home—she would miss her bright cousins and the station, and felt strangely unwilling to return to her old life.

After breakfast on Saturday morning, she went to the

horse paddock to say goodbye to Diamond and Creamy. "I'll miss you, Creamy," she murmured to the filly, "I wish I could keep you always."

She sighed and hurried back to the house, for the Newcastle train, leaving Aruntoora at ten-past-twelve, required an early departure.

Eventually the last case was stacked into the old truck, and there was a quarter of an hour to spare before the guests need leave.

"Oh, wait a minute! There's more luggage!" Jean ran off, and Beryl, puzzled, said, "I think we have everything here." The Brownleys assumed blank looks until they heard Jean approaching the house again.

Beryl turned . . . to see the sweetest, dearest little cream filly following Jean on a lead.

"Creamy!" she gasped, not fully understanding the meaning of the foal's arrival.

"A small gift for you," explained Bob, grinning at the delight that shone out from the girl's face. "But . . . oh, gee! I can't believe it!"

"And a certain little bird told us that your chauffeur, Ron Masters, is very interested in horses, and knows a lot about them, and he has agreed to look after Creamy and teach you all he knows!"

It is impossible to describe Beryl's delight. She stammered her thanks, feeling that words could not express her gratitude.

Mrs. Brownley spoke, "There's a freight car and crate on your train, so Creamy will be quite comfortable on her journey. She must have milk and bran, and Ron Masters will collect her when he has driven you home. Your father told us of the paddock not far from your house, so everything has worked out perfectly, hasn't it?"

Bob, who had saddled Rover, was to lead Creamy to the station, and now he mounted, for time was short.

The last farewells were said, and Mrs. Wren boarded the truck. Beryl, still in a daze, asked to be allowed to sit on the back, so that she could see Creamy and talk to Bob.

She climbed up nimbly, and waved as long as she could see the house from the retreating car.

Mrs. Brownley, Jean, and the youngsters watched until their eyes ached ; at last, they turned towards the house.

" Well," said Mrs. Brownley, " I think their stay here has certainly done us all a lot of good."

12

"HERE, Diamond! Come on, girlie! Now then, don't play up!"

Jean and Bob were saddling their horses preparatory to riding into the hills to look over the cattle. From time to time this duty was performed to ensure that they were in good condition, and as it was weeks since anyone had seen them, Mr. Brownley had told his elder children to ride out that way that afternoon.

"Rover's in a nasty mood," muttered Bob, and Jean added, "Diamond's pretty fresh, too. It's the flies."

They mounted and rode through the paddocks, jumping the fences, for all the station horses were good hunters.

"Which way?" queried Jean as they landed neatly on the opposite bank of the stream.

"I think it'd be best to make for Bungoola Peak, and then work west to the Swagman," Bob advised; "Dad said they're probably near the Peak, seeing it's nearly summer."

They branched to their right and advanced into the hills, climbing higher and higher until they commanded a view of most of the surrounding countryside.

"Bob!" exclaimed Jean, "look over there! Isn't that smoke?"

"By gum! You're right! And there's something moving near it!"

Jean strained her keen eyes and said briefly, "Cattle! Stampeding!"

"They'll be trapped in the valley! Jean, fly home and bring the others, and I'll go on and inspect the damage. Oh, hurry!"

Jean turned Diamond's head and raced down the mountain side, urging the mare on with voice and heels. They dodged through dense scrub and galloped hard over the plains.

"Come on, Diamond! Keep it up!" Even in her haste, Jean marvelled once more at the horse's pace; her hooves did not seem to touch the ground as she sped on, yet she appeared to be taking her time, for her stride was long and easy.

By the time they were approaching the creek, Jean could hear Diamond's heavy breathing, but one would have thought she knew the urgency, for not once did her amazing speed slacken. They sailed over the wide stretch of water, and thundered through the paddocks, jumping even the highest fences.

Mr. Brownley, working near the men's quarters, spied his daughter and the foam-flecked mare as Diamond gathered herself for the last five-foot jump, and he advanced quickly, sensing trouble.

" Bushfire ! " Jean panted, dismounting, " cattle stampeding and nearly trapped in that valley near Mount Guardian ! "

Hardly had the first startling word escaped Jean's lips before her father sprang into the saddle of his horse standing close by, shouting to the men to follow quickly.

Mrs. Brownley, hearing the commotion, came out of the house with the youngsters, who had been assisting in the spring-cleaning, and was soon informed.

" I'll come, too," she volunteered promptly. Her husband looked at her doubtfully, but with only nine to fight the burning menace, there was need of every helper, so he agreed reluctantly.

Margaret and Frank caught their horses, thinking only of the excitement, and with good presence of mind they filled kerosene tins with drinking-water for the fire-fighters, and followed more slowly.

Diamond had recovered her breath by this time, and led the way to the fire with almost the same speed as she had shown on the downward journey.

After climbing steadily for some time, the party could smell the ominous scent of smoke, at which the horses became uneasy. " Nearly there," came from Jean, and at that moment, topping a steep rise, they saw a grey billowing cloud issuing from a depression among the hills.

" There's Bob ! " cried Jean, whose quick eyes were the first to catch sight of her brother.

The company rode nearer and picketed their horses at a safe distance before running towards the crackling flames, tearing down green branches as they ran.

" Bob ! " shouted Mr. Brownley, as he came alongside

his son. Above the crash and roar of the fire, the boy had not heard the others' approach. He turned a surprised, smutty face towards his father, who noted the red-rimmed eyes and flaming cheeks.

" Rather warm, isn't it? " the boy managed to smile, " we'll have to put it out before it gets much farther—the steers are clustering at the end of the valley." His father whistled as he remarked, " It's a good thing there's so little wind."

Beating and stamping, the workers toiled on, flanking the blaze to prevent its spread, but after an hour of heartbreaking effort they felt it to be hopeless.

Bob, every sinew strained, and desperation portrayed in every action, cried out, " With God all things are possible ! We'll beat it yet ! " To which his mother, sparing no effort herself, added a fervent " Amen ! "

Mr. Brownley followed the flames, half-suffocated with the thick air, his feet blistered as he trod the scorching ground.

" Looks pretty hopeless, Boss," Clive Richardson said at last, knowing that his words would not affect Mr. Brownley's determination to fight to the end.

" We'll stick it out," the latter replied grimly. " If only the wind would change ! "

Amid the stifling heat and blinding smoke, the weary people worked on, choking and gasping, their faces and clothes blackened beyond recognition.

The menacing blaze crept on and on, drawing nearer to the cattle who, finding themselves denied an exit from the valley, were milling desperately at the far end, and trying vainly to climb the steep side.

Driven by the breeze, the flames advanced, licking greedily at the trees, which seemed to struggle as long as they could, and then, when the fiery demon overcame them, gave up the fight and crashed to the ground.

The golden sun lost its heat and changed to crimson as it slowly descended from its lofty position. Dusk left a rim of gold and pink along the western horizon, until that, too, faded to make room for twinkling stars. From the valley radiated a crimson light as a giant topaz, set with tiny black gems that were men and gaunt trees.

Hunger pangs were troubling the party, but they had no time for such irrelevant things as food, so they fought on gamely, beating with aching arms at the burning shrubs.

The time was nearing nine o'clock when Mr. Brownley uttered an exultant shout, " The wind's changing ! " The others took up the chorus, and it echoed through the broad valley, for the flames were checked in their mad onward rush, and surged in the opposite direction.

The fire-fighters stood back and shaded their watering eyes from the glare before them. They could afford a rest now, for the flames, with the wind behind them, would be blown harmlessly over the burnt ground, and the endangered cattle saved.

They renewed their efforts and extinguished some of the smaller fires, preventing their sideways spread. At last they withdrew ; the dying fire was licking the scorched earth feebly, searching in vain for new life, only to die, exhausted, in the tomb of its own destruction.

Mr. Brownley drew a sooty handkerchief from his pocket, and wiped his face, remarking, " Whew ! That was a close shave ! " Mrs. Brownley sank to the ground, her vitality forsaking her now that the danger was past. The others stretched themselves out on the cool earth, their strength sapped, and made weak attempts at humour.

" Aren't we dirty? "

" Isn't it hot? "

" I hate to imagine what would have happened if the fire had gone right into the valley ! "

" But it didn't ! And it's a miraculous answer to prayer ! "

" Yes, the hand of the Lord was certainly in that ! "

Having regained some of their strength, the stationers decided it was time to go home. " We'll inspect the damage in the morning," said Mr. Brownley as they collected their horses and wearily retraced their steps to the house.

Away from the intense heat of the fire, they soon grew cold, and were glad of hot baths and cosy beds.

All woke late next morning, sore and stiff, but prepared to put a bright face on the matter.

After breakfast everyone rode out to the scene of the fire. They found a large patch of burnt ground, several acres in area, bereft of bush except for the trunks of three giant gums that had withstood the fierce onslaught and were standing gaunt and black against the skyline. The steers had made their escape as soon as it was safe, and were miles away.

The company trod the still smouldering ashes, scattering them with well-covered feet. " From what I saw of the cattle, I think they're all right," Mr. Brownley remarked ; " when the wind changed, I had time to watch them from a distance, and they looked as fit as ever."

" Are they ready for the sales? " asked his wife, who had only glanced at them. " Oh, yes," was the reply, " we'll have to fatten them up after Christmas, and then they'll be prime cattle."

' The sales ! ' Jean thought despairingly, ' coming nearer every day ! '

Some time later they rode back to the homestead, talking bushfire to each and everyone.

" Wasn't Black Diamond splendid yesterday? " Jean praised. " You should have seen her flying down the mountain ; I guess she *knew* she had to hurry ! "

" I saw her make nothing of those fences," her father put in, " that jump she did the day we caught her was no fluke ! "

Jean glowed at this tribute to her treasure. She and the mare were becoming more and more intimate as the days flew by : it had not taken Black Diamond long to know and understand every mood and desire, every action and word of her young mistress, and Jean was quick to learn the character, temperament, and strength of her horse.

Her horse? Yes, until the beautiful black mare should be led into the sale ring, and handed over to the highest bidder. Yet Jean knew that even when Black Diamond was sold and taken miles away from her natural home, she would still belong, in spirit, to the girl who alone had wormed her way into her very heart and had won her affection.

Early next morning, the household was astir and busy about its work. The never-ending horse training kept every hand in constant employment, for there is no limit to the knowledge that a good horse should acquire. To some, the task, unvaried from year to year, would seem monotonous, but to the Brownleys it could never become such, since each individual horse brought its many interesting incidents. Jean especially revelled in the healthy, outdoor exercise, and could never have too much of it.

This morning she sat down at her desk with even more reluctance than usual. Fine warm days were heralding an early summer—just the sort of weather that was most alluring to Jean. She opened her geography book with a little sigh, and gazed beyond the dew-sprinkled grassland to the purple, white-tipped range that was, to her, the embodiment of mystery, adventure, and romance.

With great effort, she fastened her eyes on a map of Australia, but not far away a tiny bird burst forth into song, trilling its carol on to the fresh morning breeze. Jean's eyes wandered again, and grew dreamy, but with the stern determination she resumed her study.

At last the geography was completed, and Jean turned her attention to algebra. A kookaburra, perched on a lofty gum nearby, gave vent to a hearty laugh, accompanied by his mate, and Jean's eyes lifted once more. They seemed, to the girl, to be amused at the sight of human beings wasting sunny hours poring over dry-as-dust lessons, while they were free. The kookaburras ceased their laughter, and flew away over the hills.

Jean watched them until her eyes ached, noting that the

snow, already melting under the heat of the sun, was diminishing rapidly from the peaks of the higher mountains.

Commanding all her will-power, she dropped her eyes to her sums and tried to shut out the fascinating, beckoning, world outside. By dint of extreme perseverance, she completed her lessons by dinner, and as soon as the meal was over she dashed outside to enjoy the day to the full.

The yearlings, who still retained their coltish ways, were quite a handful, and needed skilled and patient care in training. Jean found all the practice she could wish for in disciplining the frisky young horses, breaking them in and teaching them manners.

Each horse had to be tamed from his half-wild state until he was quite accustomed to humans, and then broken-in gradually to the halter, bridle, and saddle. Mr. Brownley believed that a horse's character was partly dependent on his treatment in early life, so he never showed them any signs of impatience, haste, or roughness, but let them take their time, and get used to one thing before he went on with something new.

" Hallo, Boots, old fellow ! " Jean greeted a dapple cheerily as she slipped a bridle over his head, " you're ready for a ride today ! " To which startling news, the colt responded with a friendly nudge.

Jean put the saddle on gently, waiting till he had sniffed at it and made sure that it was not harmful. She then mounted lightly and took a firm hold on the reins. Boots was suspicious of the weight on his back, and felt like bucking.

But Jean's voice, cool and calm, seemed to reassure him, for he became less restive and allowed the girl to guide him over the paddock.

" There ! " murmured Jean, dismounting, " that wasn't so bad, eh, old boy? "

The affectionate colt rubbed his little wet nose against her sleeve, and she said to herself, ' This one will do for a young child—he's very quiet, and yet willing to work.'

" Like some more, Boots? " she said aloud, and this time,

she made him circle the paddock in different paces—
walking, trotting, and cantering.

Good riding horses should walk quickly and canter
slowly, an art that is the outcome of long, hard training,
and a point that the Brownleys did not overlook. They
spent tiring though enjoyable hours perfecting every detail,
and their horses, ranking as the best in that district, were
much sought after and brought high prices.

13

SPRING had blossomed into bright Australian summer, which promised to be a very hot season. Christmas wasn't far off now—only a little more than three weeks away—and the Brownleys were feeling the first touch of excitement as they prepared for the festival.

For months Jean had been secretly teaching Black Diamond some tricks, and, intelligent as ever, the mare learnt them quickly. Jean first taught her to respond to her touch without the use of saddle or bridle. Pepper helped in this, too. Now Jean was teaching the mare to rear, buck, dance, lie down and get up, at her bidding.

They rehearsed this one hot afternoon, and with every practice Jean noticed definite improvement.

In the empty cattle paddock was an old stump of a tree. Jean led Diamond to it, and gently placed her forefeet, one at a time, on the top of the stump, repeating several times, " Up, Diamond, up ! " " Down now, girlie," she said after a while.

The mare removed her forefeet from the stump, and then Jean placed one of them on the top again, saying, " Up, Diamond, come on, up ! " Diamond obeyed readily, and the girl, praising her, commanded her to get down again. Thus the words " up " and " down " were registered on the horse's intelligent mind as signals for her to perform this action.

" Now do it yourself. Come on, up, up ! " Diamond slowly complied, and Jean rewarded her with a lump of sugar. " Now, do it again. Up, come on, up, Diamond ! " she said, and lifted the hind feet up as well. After a time, the mare mounted the stump without Jean's aid. " Come

on, old lady, for the last time. Come on, up ! " Diamond
obeyed, and Jean produced a carrot which the pupil
munched eagerly.

All this was done in strict secrecy, for Mr. Brownley
would have thought it a waste of time, if he had known.

" Now, Diamond, get wild ! Come on, really wild ! "
Diamond laid her ears flat against her neck, and reared
high, waving her forelegs in the air, and snorting fiercely.
Jean recalled a time, months ago, when she had turned her
back on the same mare, in all her wildness. It had been
the real thing then, and Jean had been a little scared of
the horse she had won to herself. How much happier they
were now ! What a difference love, understanding, and
discipline had made !

" Right, old girl, calm down ! " she ordered cheerily,
" now be afraid of me . . . go on, afraid of me ! " Diamond
retreated a little, and advanced again slowly, ears forward,
nose quivering. Jean made a movement, and the horse
darted away, to draw near once more. This was repeated
several times, until Diamond eventually came up to
Jean.

" Good work, girlie," praised Jean, " you'd make an
excellent circus pony." Her heart grew cold as she said
it, as once again, she realized the awful truth. The sale of
the stock was to be held in early February, and after that
she would never see Diamond again. Jean stroked the
glossy neck and murmured with a catch in her voice, " Oh,
Black Diamond, why did I fall in love with you so ? Just
to have this happiness for a few months? "

A hot tear rolled down to the tip of her nose, and she
brushed it off quickly. Diamond answered as best she
could by whinnying and nuzzling the girl affectionately.
Jean pulled herself together and said, " Oh, well, that'll be
enough for today, Diamond. We'll go back to the others."

Diamond had grown even since her capture, and stood
more than sixteen hands high. " I think she's come from
better stock than the brumbies," Mr. Brownley had
remarked often as he had inspected the mare, " she may

have been lost, and joined the herd ; or her ancestors may have done so."

Certainly Black Diamond was perfect in build, carriage, movement ; in fact, in everything—too good for a wild horse. Wherever she went, she stepped lightly, carrying herself with graceful ease that was a pleasure to behold. Her rippling muscles developed beneath her shining coat : she was dainty, yet powerful ; gentle, yet spirited ; and in Jean's eyes, there was no horse to equal her.

The Brownleys could not afford their annual before-Christmas trip to Brisbane this year, and so they were all busy making their presents.

Joe Wood had shown the youngsters how to carve models, and Margaret, especially, showed great adaptability. Frank was too clumsy to bring his work to perfection.

Joe proved to be a conscientious worker, and very good with horses. In his spare time he shut himself away and carved : it was the only art in which he excelled, and he now made the most of it.

Mr. Brownley was cutting and sewing leather, and nailing wood. Mrs. Brownley was sewing, knitting, cooking and helping her husband, and, of course, there was the traditional thrill of all hands on the station stirring the Christmas pudding.

Bob and Jean were drawing, painting, cutting, fitting, and many other things, and the house was constantly filled with simmering excitement.

One evening the stock of streamers was taken from the jumble in one of the cupboards, and the family spent their free hours sorting out each paper chain from the tangled mass. When at last this was completed, plain streamers were interlaced to form more attractive decorations. Some rather dilapidated paper bells and lanterns were touched up and hung in places of honour above the doors. The streamers, made as pretty as possible, were draped just under the ceilings and around the walls.

Excitement seethed and bubbled over as Christmas Day drew near, and last-minute preparations were performed.

The children were secretly arranging a special entertainment, and enlisted the help of Bob and Jean. They had taught the dogs many tricks, and had learnt songs and recitations. Jean had her own surprise which she decided to use in this, for Black Diamond had made great progress with her tricks, and was fit for exhibition. Bob had a book of magician's tricks, and with the help of Frank he rehearsed them for the party.

Lessons were now completely in the background, conveniently pushed out of the way of the less tedious Christmas tasks.

At last, after what seemed like years, Christmas Eve arrived. Final touches were added to the various presents, and Jean and Bob worked hard to finish hand-painted Christmas cards.

The great day dawned, and the Brownleys awoke to enjoy the festival to the full. Mrs. Brownley stretched luxuriously, and looked out of the window. Hark! What was that? Increasing in volume, a strain of " Christians Awake " floated out upon the still air.

Mr. Brownley roused as the tune changed to that of " Good King Wenceslas ". " They're men's voices," murmured his wife, and craned her neck, to see the five stationhands singing gaily.

The younger members of the household were leaning out of the windows of their two bedrooms, joining in the chorus.

" Happy Christmas, Boss! Happy Christmas, Missus! Happy Christmas, all! " the men called out as they approached the verandah.

" Thank you, everyone ! " Mr. Brownley responded with warmth, " and the same to all of you ! " His wife chimed in, " This is a lovely surprise : we *do* appreciate it ! "

Each man carried a large parcel containing their gifts, and they handed them through the window amid much talk and banter.

Milking was done as soon as possible, while Mrs. Brownley prepared a special breakfast. The hungry people, including the hands, seated themselves around the gaily-decorated table, and fell to with eagerness.

Rump steak, eggs, and onions filled them with satisfaction. They drank their tea with the same delight, surveying the streamer-bedecked table, and joking noisily.

Many hands made light work of the washing-up, a job which even the youngsters liked when it was flavoured with such jolly excitement.

When order was restored once more, Mrs. Brownley, assisted by her family, stuffed two fowls and seasoned roast pork. These were put in the oven, and the stationers went to church for the Christmas service held there annually.

As the party trotted down the mountain side, they broke into carols. Joe had heard them when he had occasionally been in the city for Christmas, but he had never tried to pick them up, so was not always able to join in with the singing.

After an hour's riding, they approached the little church. The Gilmores were deep in conversation with the minister, and the Edwards family chatted with some other neighbours.

The Brownley household was greeted joyously, and amid friendly gossip, they went into the church. Margaret and Frank joined a small group of children and sat near the front, excitedly whispering and fidgeting. The stationers occupied two of the small pews, and made up a quarter of the congregation.

Joe had accompanied the others to the church on previous Sundays, and before that he had heard fragments of the Gospel at open-air meetings, but not once had he listened to a Christmas message as delivered by the minister there.

The people listened with eager interest as he retold the wonderful story of Christ's birth, and the more wonderful reason for His coming down to earth.

When the service had drawn to a close, the congregation sauntered out of the church, and gradually divided to go to the various homes.

" That's one of the best Christmas addresses I've heard," Mrs. Brownley commented, and the others all agreed. " I like Mr. Marsh. He's open and frank, and what he says rings true."

The horses cantered slowly along the dusty track, and mustered their forces for the climb ahead. Jean was riding Pepper, for she felt that he was being a little left out. Black Diamond was beautiful and magnificent, and presented all that could be desired, but Pepper had been faithful and loving, and had shared many years with Jean.

" Teddy's dog has three pups now—the old airedale." Frank spoke of the Gilmores' younger son. " They're beauties, he reckons."

" And Jack," Margaret added, " says that he's going to have one of this year's colts ! "

" Gee ! Poor kid ! He's nearly twelve, and we all got our horses when we were seven ! "

The company thundered over a bridge that spanned a rippling, sparkling stream. Farther up the creek, the riders halted their steeds for a drink, for the hill was steep, and the journey long.

At last, the homestead was reached, and Mrs. Brownley hurried in to the kitchen to complete the dinner preparations. The girls rubbed their horses down, and followed their mother to assist in the task of feeding eleven hungry mouths.

The fowls were sizzling merrily in their bed of fat. Jean sniffed as she entered the hot kitchen, and licked her lips in anticipation. " Gee, Mum ! " exclaimed her sister, " I'm ravenous ! "

Mrs. Brownley surveyed the roast potatoes, and Jean, at the sight of the tempting red-brown skins, remarked joyfully, " My ! No one can cook like you, Mum ! " The other vegetables were equally appetising, and the girls became impatient to sample them. " Isn't it ready yet, Mum? " the boys asked again and again as they hovered hopefully around the oven. Then Mrs. Brownley would shake her head, and send them off to do some job.

At long last the bell was rung, and the men filed in from verandah and garden. The day was, perhaps, the hottest of the season, but the steaming dinner was devoured hungrily.

" I've got a wish-bone ! " Frank cried excitedly, " here you are, Mum ! "

Together, they hooked their little fingers round each end, and tugged. Snap ! The bone had broken, and the wish went to Frank, who laughed, " I wish we had a Christmas dinner every day ! "

Then Joe discovered the other wishbone, and following Frank's example, he broke it with Mr. Brownley, who got the wish. " Well, I wish you all a very happy Christmas and New Year," he said with sincerity.

" My word, Missus, you can cook ! " Max Weston mumbled heartily between mouthfuls. This was the general opinion of the hands, as the first course disappeared.

The dishes were cleared away while Mrs. Brownley extracted the all-important Christmas pudding from the pot. It was quickly served to each plate—rich brown, and piping hot.

The people nearly burnt their mouths as they consumed it. Care had to be taken here, for many silver charms, almost as old as Bob, were embedded cosily in the pudding.

" I've got a bell ! "

" Look ! A horse-shoe ! "

" I've found a bachelor's button ! "

" Here's a shilling ! " were only some of the delighted cries that followed each other in rapid succession.

Amid much merriment the company attacked the overflowing fruit bowl and dainty dishes of sweets and nuts.

Eventually, the feast was concluded. Everyone—even the children—declared themselves absolutely full, and rose to help clear away the remains of the sumptuous meal.

Then the party repaired to the shade of the gums for a brief ' siesta ' before the activities of the afternoon.

" My, I'm hot ! " sighed Bob, as he lay full length on the grass.

" So am I," Jean echoed. " Come and have a dip in the creek to cool us down." The pair summoned the energy to run off, followed closely by the youngsters. After a while, they emerged from their rooms clad in bathing-suits, and raced towards the creek through the horse paddock.

Plunging in at one of the pools deep enough for swimming, Bob swam to the far side and announced the water to be delightfully cold. Jean and Frank jumped in, and Margaret crawled out to a low, overhanging branch and dangled her legs in the water.

" Come on," urged Bob, " shake a leg, Margaret ! "

" That's what I am doing," the girl returned, swinging her legs vigorously. Splash ! Her slender form shot downwards and disappeared beneath the surface of the pool. Frank chuckled wickedly, but was instantly ducked when his victim reappeared.

" Race you to the other end," challenged Jean, and the four churned the water in their effort to outdo each other. Bob and Jean reached a certain jutting rock simultaneously, with Margaret and Frank only inches behind. They clambered on to the rock, sunning themselves and then waded upstream to another pool not so deep as the first.

Finally Jean said, " Let's go back now. We'll have to start our entertainment soon." So the four climbed out on to the bank and dried themselves in the sun, before running to the homestead to change.

The effects of the dinner had worn off by now, and the people were looking around for some amusement. Bob went to his mother's side and whispered in her ear. Then the four hurried inside to gather the material for the performance.

Giggling nervously, the youngsters walked as sedately as possible out of the house, and bowed to the audience. Margaret gabbled an introduction : " On behalf of myself, and the rest of the company, I extend to you Christmas greetings . . . er . . . er . . . and hope that you are enjoying this . . . er . . . festive season. For your entertainment, we now present to you . . . er . . . some items rendered entirely by our own members."

She bowed again, and Frank tittered. " Our first item,"

he grinned, " is a duet, sung by me and Margaret." They proceeded to sing a round of carols, grinning from ear to ear, and occasionally giggling. From time to time, the older children winced, for the youngsters were not musical, and paid little respect to the right tune.

They ended the last carol, bowed once more, and retreated amid laughing applause.

Then Jean came on, wearing a long dress which Mrs. Brownley recognized as a discarded working frock. A battered felt hat adorned her head, and a pair of gum-boots did justice for shoes. Her mouth was down at the corners as she gave the title of her piece in solemn, warning tones : " The Death of Little Willie."

The audience smiled and settled down to listen.

" Now Willie was a little boy . . .
    A little boy was he . . .

She stopped and looked round at Bob, saying in a loud whisper, " Heh ! What comes next ? " Amid the laughter, Bob returned, " Something about being four-foot-three ! "

" Ah ! " the girl continued happily, " I've got it ! Something about being four-foot-three ! "

Her audience roared, and she proceeded to relate the woeful tale of a foolish little boy who ate too much at a party.

" And when he got home, he felt so sick,
    His mother put him to bed.
    He moaned and groaned, and started to hick,
    And now—poor Willie is dead ! "

Jean pulled out a handkerchief and mopped her eyes.

" So this is the moral, my cherished friend,
    It makes the story complete.
    If you moan and groan, you're near the end,
    When you've had too much to eat ! "

Amid a roar of applause, she bowed and made her exit, whereupon the youngsters approached with Ruffles, Barney, and Scamp.

"We," announced Margaret, bowing low, "are the Famous Five . . ."

A titter ran through the rows of listeners before them as Mr. Brownley murmured, "The Notorious Nippers, more like it!"

". . . presenting for your enjoyment Ten Tip-top Tricks taught by the Troublesome Two!"

First on the list was jumping through an old iron hoop. The dogs lined up and went through the paces excellently. The youngsters joined hands and Ruffles bounded over. Just as he landed, however, he spied a rabbit some distance away. Like a shot from a gun, he gave chase, with Barney and Scamp joining in, yelping madly. Vainly the party called them, until Mr. Brownley caught them and brought them back.

The youngsters, red in the face, went through the performance again, this time, without interruption. The various tricks were the result of much patient training, and the audience was fully satisfied as it watched the antics of the dogs.

"Now we come to our final item." Bob walked forward with a table, and Frank followed with sundry interesting articles. Jean laughed to herself, and thought, "If they only knew what the final item really is!"

A black cloth was draped over an old box on which some handkerchiefs, small boxes, a hat, a pair of gloves, a tumbler, and various other articles, were arranged.

Dressed in old cloaks of red, green, and brown, Bob placed himself behind the table and announced that he was "Horace Hickleback, the World Renowned Magician," but Frank, with only a high hat and gum-boots over his shorts, seemed to lessen the dignity of the announcement.

"The first thing I will show you is this . . ."—he held up a red handkerchief. "I will change it to blue. Gustavia, bring hither the basket." Frank complied, and Bob, after proving the basket to be empty, placed the handkerchief in it, murmuring "Abracadabra"—at which Frank giggled—and drew out a blue cloth.

The watchers cheered, and Frank took the handkerchief to put away. Alas! He held it too carelessly, for a breeze blew it up, enabling the audience to see both sides—one red and one blue!

Horace Hickleback glossed this over by hurrying on with the next trick. " I now will produce an egg from this hat," he said, removing Frank's headgear. " See? It's quite empty." He held the hat so that his sleeve rested on the brim, and, lo and behold! A brown egg appeared in the hat.

" Now, I will make it disappear again," boasted Bob. He tilted the hat slightly, but the egg, obstinate as it was, merely hovered on the brim and fell to the ground, a slimy mess.

The memory of Bob's face never failed, thereafter, to bring a laugh to the lips of those watching.

Some minutes before the close of the ' programme ', Jean slipped away almost unnoticed, and Bob thought, " She could at least have stayed till I'd finished." He had just completed his last trick, and was about to declare the concert closed, when footsteps were heard coming from behind the house. The audience gasped, and Bob looked round to see a sight he would never forget.

Jean approached, clad in her neat grey jodhpurs, her hair loose and bedecked with ribbons, and close behind, following faithfully without a lead, stepped Black Diamond, more beautiful than the company had ever seen her. Her coat shone like a polished floor, and her hooves were gleaming ebony. Adorning her arched neck, her mane, and her tail, were ribbons of every hue, and as she stood, proudly erect, with tossing head and coat of sheen, her beauty robbed the spectators of speech.

Jean advanced and announced, " We have now come to the final item on our programme. Black Diamond is going to give you a short performance. Come on, Diamond." She turned round and murmured, " Now, old lady, do your stuff ! "

Diamond stepped forward slowly, and Jean said loudly,

" Now, Diamond, do you want to do some tricks for the people? " The beautifully plumed head nodded without hesitation.

" All right, then, bow to them. Come on, girlie, bow ! " Slowly, one foreleg was bent as the mare's body tilted forward, and then upright again. The audience were dumbfounded, and Jean continued, " Now, girlie, show them how you waltz."

Black Diamond, her ears sharply pricked, circled slowly around the girl, imitating a dancing step, occasionally turning completely around. The eyes of horse and girl seemed never to leave each other, and as Jean surreptitiously nodded her head, the mare dropped clumsily to the ground.

" Oh ! You fell over ! You can't waltz properly yet. Come on, Diamond, get up ! " Black Diamond rose obediently, and nosed her young mistress. " Now, Diamond, let's pretend you're a wild horse. You've got to be frightened of me. Come on, show me how you do it. Come on, old lady, be frightened of me."

Black Diamond turned tail and galloped away, to approach hesitatingly again. Jean waved her arm, and the horse started and retreated quickly. As before, this was repeated a few times until Diamond had reached the girl.

" Now, Diamond, get wild with me," and the mare flattened her ears and snapped. " Come on, *really* wild ! " Black Diamond reared high, pawing the air and screaming. After doing this three times, she lowered her head and lifted her hind-feet into the air.

" All right, girlie, calm down," ordered Jean ; " and now, show me what you can do with this." Diamond went behind the indicated box, and pushed it into the centre of the ring with her forefeet. Then she slowly mounted it and stood there while the audience clapped vigorously.

" Down now, old girl," and when Diamond had obeyed, Jean jumped on to her bare back. " Ladies and gentlemen, I sincerely hope you have enjoyed our little effort this afternoon, and I trust it has added to the festivity of the

season. Bow to the people, Diamond!" The horse complied, and Jean, still standing, perfectly balanced, on
Diamond's back, rode out amid a storm of applause.

"Jean! That was wonderful! I've never seen anything like it." Bob greeted her, and Jean and Black
Diamond were quickly surrounded with a band of wondering, enthusiastic admirers, who exclaimed and questioned
till the girl felt tongue-tied. The last item was certainly
the hit of the programme, though the others were warmly
praised, and Jean felt that this was ample reward for the
long, patient work that she and Diamond had shared.

By this time it was five o'clock, and the company's
thoughts turned towards the tea-table. Jean rode Black
Diamond to the horse paddock, where she removed the
trappings and set down an extra feed of oats with a little
bran mash.

"Diamond, old lady, you couldn't have done better,
and I couldn't be more proud of you! Oh, girlie! I love
you more every minute, and I'm sure you love me; I can
see it in your eye. Oh, what shall we do when we're
parted?" The reaction of the day's merriment descended
on Jean in full force, and she was full of gloom. ' No good
moping,' she thought, making a gallant effort to shake it
off, and giving the mare a final caress she ran back to the
house.

The large kitchen table creaked under the weight of
mince pies, salads, jellies, fruit and cream—indeed, there
was no room for another thing as the stationers seated
themselves. In true Christmas style they devoured the
dainties until the plates were bare, and then Mr. Brownley
opened the family Bible.

In the midst of the festivity, they did not forget to come
for their spiritual food and to spend some time in com-
munion with the Lord. But this was not the only time
that they had contact with Him, for in every moment of
their lives the fellowship of their Father was with them.

At last the remnants of the meal were disposed of, and
the party gathered on the verandah to unwrap their presents

in the dusk. This seemed the most important part of the day, and seething with excitement and anticipated pleasure, the people seated themselves beside their pile of presents.

Mr. Brownley received a stockwhip, a pair of breeches, a pair of slippers, and various articles dear to a man's heart. His wife was given a leather jacket and jodhpurs for the cold days, a picture painted specially by Jean, and a dainty handkerchief box, among other things. Bob was delighted with a book on surgery, which had arrived by post some days previously, and a polished saddle for Rover. Jean was awed by an exquisitely carved model of Black Diamond, presented by Joe, and sundry things for herself and the horse ; while the youngsters were completely satisfied with books and riding material. The station hands received their gifts, thoughtfully chosen by the Boss for their enjoyment.

The last red glow faded from the sky, and a twinkling, silver light appeared. The people were tired after their long and busy day, and it was decided that the time for bed had come.

So the stationers, weary but happy, wished each other good night and retired to their rooms, where they were soon slumbering peacefully.

14

" HEIGH-HO, heigh-ho ! It's off to work we go ! "
Jean sang lustily as she walked arm-in-arm with
Bob to the horse paddock. Once more she was at the peak
of excitement, for the cattle had to be brought in for the
sales and fattened up and cared for for many weeks.

Jean saddled Black Diamond, and mounting, followed her
father on the upward climb ; the only thing that marred
her happiness was the constant reminder that soon she was
to lose the horse she loved above all others.

The youngsters, much to their delight, had persuaded
their parents to let them help with the mustering, and now
they gaily raced ahead, chasing each other and sending back
jovial taunts to the " snails ", who took the teasing good-
naturedly.

" Your horses will be tired out before we reach the steers,"
Mr. Brownley remonstrated, " you'd better go slow now ;
you'll need all your energy when we get there." Margaret
and Frank made a gallant effort to ride soberly by their
father, and succeeded until the mountains rose around and
above them.

" We'll start near the Peak, and work back to the Swagman," Mr. Brownley advised ; " they're possibly near the
Peak."

So they turned to the right and ascended steadily towards

the highest elevation on the Brownleys' property—Bungoola Peak. "Not here," muttered Bob as his eyes roved among hill and dale. They rode slowly along the short cuts—narrow ridges and deep, rocky ravines, scrutinizing the countryside as they rode.

"There they are!" Frank exclaimed as they picked their way up the steep slope of a mossy gorge—Gipsies' Glen—and emerged into brilliant sunlight once more. The others screwed up their eyes and picked out the herd of steers grazing peacefully on a distant hillside.

As they approached, Mr. Brownley did some mental calculation and said, "We'll have to take them through the gully and around the Swagman."

They spread out in a fan-like formation behind the steers, who glared balefully at them and trotted quickly down the hillside and through the broad gully.

"That was easy!" laughed Jean, "they were just in the right position."

"Don't be optimistic," her father cautioned, "the fun and games will start when we get into the open country."

His words proved to be true, for when the herd emerged from the gully into the comparative freedom of the more open slopes, they became restless. Mr. Brownley looked at his daughter and remarked, "We must watch them now."

They jogged along in the hot afternoon sunlight, constantly on the alert for any signs of straying from the path. Just as they sighted the Swagman, its nearer side cut clean and rising sheer from the ground which was strewn with rocks—the reminder of a recent landslide—one of the leaders broke away and raced towards the other side.

Jean, who was flanking the herd on the right, wheeled Diamond sharply and gave chase. But the steer was not going to submit to captivity: he lengthened his stride and pounded over the broken ground in a desperate bid for freedom.

Diamond warmed to the fray and galloped easily after him, shortening the distance between them at every stride.

Crack! Jean's stockwhip was flourished and reported loudly in the still air.

The steer dodged to the right, but the mare was too quick for him. The whip cracked over his head—he wheeled round the way he had come, and Jean piloted him back triumphantly.

"Nice work, Jean," her father commented as they resumed their homeward journey. Guarding the cattle closely, they described a semi-circle around the Swagman, and took the track over the hills and across the stream.

The steers gave some trouble, but were handled expertly, and it was not long before they were guided to the gate of the first paddock. Here, however, some showed a keen dislike of entering, and much hard work was necessary. The horses, perfectly trained, obeyed their riders nobly, so that after some little time, the steers were all safely through.

Eventually, they were forced through another four gates and ushered into a large grassy paddock. Fodder and water were supplied, and the others came out to inspect them as they settled down to that all-important work—eating.

There were twelve in all, year-old sons of the few cows that had not eaten the dread poison weed which had carried off more than half the Brownleys' breeding herd. There were eight heifers, too, not so far out, which were to be sold, and as there was still some time before tea, Mr. Brownley decided to bring them in.

Accompanied by Bob, he rode out near Ghost Cavern, and found them there. They gave little trouble, and were soon munching contentedly in the paddock adjacent to the steers.

"Green's Butchery will be pleased with these," remarked Mr. Brownley, nodding towards the latter, "but they need plenty of good feed before they look their best." He looked across his shoulder to where three bull calves, born late, were growing fat on grass and corn, and added, "They'll bring a good price, too."

For the next few days, horses and cattle received unusual attention. They were fed and groomed and almost nursed.

All hands were busy training the yearlings and erstwhile brumbies to perfection, concentrating especially on the hurdlers ; Mr. Brownley expected to get a good price for them, since hunters were in great demand. With his wife he spent many an evening discussing the brumbies and how they were an answer to prayer, hoping that they might even restore the family to its former prosperity.

Jean passed all her spare time with Black Diamond, telling the mare of her troubles, and seeking comfort in her presence.

The sale was to be held on the last Friday in January ; it had been advertised in the papers, and many prospective buyers were anticipated, for the Brownleys' station was famous for its high standard and excellent quality stock.

Thursday found Jean moody and restless, and unable to study. Mrs. Brownley understandingly granted her a " holiday ", and the girl flew out to Black Diamond. She flung her arms around the horse's neck, and leaning her head against the mane, sobbed, broken-heartedly.

" Oh, Diamond ! Dear old Diamond ! They can't take you away from me ! " The mare softly snorted and nuzzled her mistress affectionately. Jean tried hard to master her rebellion, and prayed desperately, " O, God ! Please, *please* don't let her be sold ! "

And then, with a flash of insight, she realized that her will was not being wholly submitted to her Lord, and while she was in this state He could not hold perfect sway over her heart. The rebellion left her, as she humbly prayed again, " Lord, if it be Thy will, please let me keep Diamond, but if it is not Thy will . . . " Jean bowed her head in utter submission—she had fought her battle, and conquered ; but it was a hard-won, costly victory.

From that moment, a great peace stole over her heart, and though Diamond's silky mane was damped with salty tears, Jean faced the morrow with a calm, faithful hope, knowing that whatever happened was only for her final good.

Friday dawned, and the stationers rose even earlier than

usual, for last-minute preparations filled all their time. Mr. Brownley had engaged an auctioneer from a town some distance down the line, and he had arrived the day before to inspect the animals, for the sale was to be held on the property. People from far and near would soon be gathering on the grass not far from the house, for Mr. Brownley was popular among his neighbours. Helped by the men, he rigged up the huge marquee and tiers of benches that were used for the annual sales. Margaret and Frank got themselves into mischief by scrambling under the canvas and over the benches.

Above the excitement and bustle, a hot sun, pouring down its rays, promised a ' scorcher ', and Jean would have enjoyed the event to the full had it not been for the sorrow that clouded her horizon. She worked hard, grooming the horses, in an effort to forget it, but her mind was constantly filled with it.

At last she came to Black Diamond, whom she groomed with all the tenderness of her overwhelming emotions. She curry-combed her neck and murmured, " Well, old lady, I guess this is the last time I'll be doing this." She stopped abruptly, reproving herself. Where was her faith? Hadn't she prayed long and earnestly about it? She continued, filled with new hope and new faith.

Mr. Brownley, passing by and glancing at the two, almost relented from selling the mare ; but the money was needed urgently, and, besides, Jean must learn some time that she could not have everything she wished for in this world. Still, he found it hard to deny his daughter her heart's desire. He had listed Black Diamond last on the catalogue, so that Jean could have her as long as possible, and also because she would be the greatest sale of the day.

People were now arriving in buggies and drays, eager to make good purchases. The animals were gathered into adjoining paddocks, and lined up in order. Mr. Stedman, the auctioneer, a peppery, red-faced little man, stood alertly on his rostrum, hammer in hand, and when all the buyers were assembled, the sale was opened without delay.

The cattle, really the minor item, were to be sold first ; as soon as the people had settled, Dick Harris led in one of the three bull calves, and bidding began immediately. It was finally handed over to a burly farmer, and the second and third were sold after some heated bidding, for those who knew the good points of cattle were anxious to possess one of these. Then the heifers and steers were auctioned, and, as was expected, Mr. Green, a prosperous butcher from the bordering wheatlands, purchased all the steers and took no further interest in the sale.

The cattle dispensed with, Joe Wood brought on the first brumby mare and foal. Mr. Stedman declared their good points, and encouraged the already high bidding. Mr. Brownley, sitting near the auctioneer and jotting down the price of each sale in a notebook, felt his hopes rise as the day proceeded, for the bidding reached a height that even he had not dreamed possible. The hunters, being in great demand at that time, brought very high prices that sent a prayer of thanksgiving to his lips.

At half-past ten, there was a fifteen-minute break for morning tea served on trestle tables. Jean had to leave Black Diamond to help her mother, but as soon as the visitors were returning to the marquee, and the washing-up was done, she hurried back to the paddock so that she would not lose one possible moment of the horse's company.

As soon as the seats were filled again, Mr. Stedman continued the auction, his rasping voice sounding harsh on the hot morning air.

The youngsters, being quite used to this annual event, soon tired of the inactivity, and scrambled under the canvas in search of a diversion. Some of the children who had come with their parents, had also left their mothers' sides, and were playing an enthusiastic game of hide-and-seek. Margaret and Frank joined in, choosing all the best hiding-places, and exasperating the seekers.

" What'll we do now? " asked a small, flaxen-haired girl of about eight. Frank's eyes wandered over the heads of the children to where the numerous horses, free of their buggies, were grazing or resting, and a gleam came into his eye.

" Let's see who can harness a horse the quickest," he suggested. The others agreed delightedly, and the competitors, ranging in age from eight to thirteen, took up their positions ready to catch their horses.

" Go ! " shouted Margaret, and instantly the playground became a scene of scurry and confusion as the somewhat bewildered horses were caught, pushed between the shafts, and harnessed rapidly. Drowsy with the heat of the sun, they gave little trouble, and allowed themselves to be pushed and pulled, while the children, with expert deftness, strapped and buckled until a boy of eleven dashed up to a certain gum tree, declaring triumphantly, " I've won ! "

They unharnessed the horses, and started the second relay. Margaret and Frank came first and second, proving how well they had been trained.

" Let's put them in backwards," suggested Margaret, when the patient horses had been freed once more. Frank chuckled gleefully as he caught a wiry dun and harnessed him quickly before leading him, head first, between the shafts.

Shouts of laughter escaped the children as they watched the dun's face—a mixture of puzzlement and sleepy tolerance.

" Now we'll make him go," chortled Margaret, placing a handful of chaff, gathered from a nose-bag, in the cart. The horse stretched his neck in a vain effort to reach it, and took a step forward, and another, and another, until he had pushed the cart hard against an old buggy.

The children were nearly doubled up with laughter, but presently a nine-year-old girl protested, " He's our horse ! Let him out, the poor thing ! " Margaret and Frank good-humouredly unbuckled the straps and gave the dun the tantalizing chaff as a reward for the entertainment.

" Let's go and see how many mares have been sold," suggested Margaret as she and Frank scampered towards the marquee.

As they passed close to the paddock where the horses were waiting, they saw Jean, leaning her head on Diamond's neck, and a pang of remorse shot through them. They felt it out of place to have been so carefree and jolly, and Frank murmured, " Poor old Jean ! I wish we could help her ! " They continued on their way, suddenly subdued, and peeping through the opening of the marquee, were just in time to hear the hammer's final blow as a bad-tempered mare and foal were sold.

Out in the paddock, Jean and Black Diamond talked to each other in a language that only horse lovers understand. The mare, quick to sense Jean's sorrow, gave all her sympathy in a way that only horses do. " Dear old Diamond ! " the girl muttered, " there never was a horse like you ! "

The announcement of a half-hour break for dinner cut across her words, and with reluctance, she climbed over the fence and hurried towards the house to help her mother. Jean usually helped to prepare the dinner, but today she had not noticed the passing of the time, and was guiltily surprised when she found it ready. Mrs. Brownley had understandingly left her with Diamond, and enlisted the aid of the youngsters. Jean made amends as best she could by serving the visitors and washing up after the meal.

The buyers regathered in the marquee and waited eagerly for the yearling sales, which would occupy the whole afternoon. The brumby yearlings were brought in first, and went for prices so high that Mr. and Mrs. Brownley, sitting together near the auctioneer, felt their hopes rise beyond expectancy, and thanked God for His wonderful provision for their need.

" I don't know what we would have done without that herd of brumbies," Mr. Brownley remarked, " it was certainly a glorious answer to prayer that Jean saw them in the valley."

" Yes, it was indeed," his wife agreed, and paused before she added, " John, is it absolutely necessary that Black Diamond be sold? She means so much to Jean, and she's proved her worth to us more than once."

Mr. Brownley frowned as he answered hesitatingly, "Well, . . . oh, I don't know. I hate to refuse the girl anything . . . but, for myself, I'm afraid that this love of horses will become an obsession with her ; wait a moment, what was that? Grey colt, sold for five hundred guineas ! That's not bad, is it? And I want to break her of it."

"You won't," cut in his wife, speaking from experience, "you should know yourself that no one can quench the love of true horse-lovers."

"Well, p'r'aps so, but still, there are plenty of horses on the station besides Black Diamond."

Mrs. Brownley sighed as she replied, "John, you are very practical, and you can't understand why people go crazy over one particular horse. But I know—I've done it—when I was eighteen. There was a horse next to Dad's sheep-run—a beauty, chestnut with black legs, and I fell utterly in love with him the first day he came. He got a fever one cold winter, and died, and I've never forgotten him."

Mr. Brownley was silent for a while, contemplating.

"Anyway," his wife continued, "I've been praying about it for a long time, and I know that, if it's God's will, He will somehow prevent Diamond's sale, or return her to us."

The hours crept by slowly, until it was three o'clock, and time for afternoon tea. Jean left Black Diamond again and spread the trestle tables with plates of cakes and biscuits.

The visitors arranged themselves around the long tables and drank cups of tea carried out to them. The youngsters scampered off when their duty was done, and Mrs. Brownley, Bob, and Jean, helped by the hands, attacked the washing-up while the diners made their way to the marquee once more.

Eventually, the last cup was put away, and Jean was free to spend her last moments with Black Diamond. She hastened to the paddock where the remaining ten yearlings were lined up, noting on her way that some of the buyers, content with their purchases, were preparing to go home. She advanced towards the fence and scanned the paddock for Diamond. But she saw no trim, black shape, heard no joyful, welcoming whinny, for Black Diamond was gone !

Jean's heart missed several beats. Had she been sold already? The girl glanced into the tent to see a bay colt being paraded, and murmured, " She can't have been sold ! She's last to be offered."

The bay was sold, and Max Weston led him out to the paddock again. Jean climbed over the fence and asked quickly, " Max, where's Diamond? "

Max's puzzled face was sufficient answer as he replied, " I don't know, Miss Jean. The Boss was watching the horses, and there were plenty of people around, so I went away for a moment, and when I came back, the people were all in the tent and Diamond was gone ! "

" Max ! " Jean gasped. " Surely . . . she couldn't have been stolen ! "

" I don't know what's become of her," the man answered, nonplussed, " but I don't see how she could have been stolen. I couldn't tell the Boss while I was leading Bayside around ! "

" I'll tell him now," said Jean as she ran through the opening and up to her father's seat. " Dad ! " she breathed, " Diamond's gone ! "

Bob sprang to his feet, but his father said, " You stay here, Bob, and take down the prices while I look for her." Mr. Brownley's face was working as he handed his note-book to Bob, and followed Jean outside.

They ran round to the paddock, but the mare was still not there. Mr. Brownley scanned the horizon, but no trace of Black Diamond was to be found.

" Would anyone steal her? " Jean wondered, but her father answered, " I don't think so : there are too many people around, and the horses weren't left on their own long enough."

" P'r'aps she just went off by herself," suggested the girl, " she could easily jump that fence, and maybe she had watched the other horses, and knew what was coming to her." Again Mr. Brownley was doubtful.

" I don't think she could know," he said, " but still, she's very intelligent, and may have guessed that she was to be taken away."

They searched again, and finally Mr. Brownley said, " We'll have to find her. Jean, take Rover out towards Bungoola Peak. I'll have to send two men down the road in case she has been stolen." So saying, he returned to the marquee to take Bob's place, for it was essential for him to remain on the scene.

Jean sped to the horse paddock to catch Rover. Mrs. Brownley followed more slowly, and, saddling her gelding, Peter, she took the path to the Swagman.

Jean galloped over the hills and upwards to the Peak, scouring the bush in vain. " There are so many hiding-places here," she thought, " that she could be right under my nose and I wouldn't see her." She worked westward and reaching the summit of a steep hill, she saw a tiny dark speck not far from the Swagman. It was her mother, cantering Peter in and out through the network of hills and gullies.

" It's pretty hopeless," Jean muttered, " we'll never find her here ! " She wheeled her mount and descended by a different track, keeping her eyes open for any signs of the missing horse.

Meanwhile, in the marquee, Mr. Brownley waited rest-lessly. Six yearlings had been auctioned, and there were only three more. What had happened to Black Diamond? Where was she? Had the others found her yet?

Another horse was sold, and still the black mare had not returned. Mr. Brownley's ears caught the sound of galloping hooves, approaching the marquee, but it was only Bob returning from a fruitless search. A cream colt was being paraded as the boy showed an anxious face from the opening before disappearing again to continue the hunt.

One by one, the seekers returned, their quarry still un-found. The news spread like wildfire until all in the marquee knew of Black Diamond's mysterious disappearance.

The last yearling, a roan filly, was brought in, and Mr. Brownley became desperate. And then, suddenly he remembered his wife's words, " I've been praying about it for a long time, and I know that, if it's God's will, He will somehow prevent Diamond's sale, or return her to us." Was this God's answer to the prayer of His children?

Mr. Stedman's voice boomed out over the crowd. " Nine fifty I'm bid ! Any more for this beautiful little filly? One thousand ! Eleven hundred ! Any advance on eleven hundred? Come on, any advance? Eleven fifty ! Eleven fifty guineas to that man in the corner . . . going, going, gone ! "

The filly was led out and Mr. Stedman continued, " Now, Mr. Brownley, is the mare found yet? " To the man's negative reply, he said, " I'm sorry, ladies and gentlemen, the mare has been missing since afternoon recess, and has not turned up yet. She should be found shortly."

They waited for some time, but still Black Diamond did not put in an appearance. " If she isn't here soon," the auctioneer said at last, " I will have to close the sale." He was impatient to return to town, and finally he announced, " Ladies and gentlemen, the mare has not been found yet, so she is withdrawn from sale. The sale is now closed. Good afternoon, ladies and gentlemen."

The buyers rose and made their exit, talking excitedly and yet disappointedly of the incident, for many had hoped to buy the already famous mare, and others were interested in the price she would have fetched.

The people were not anxious to go home, as, for most of them, the annual sales meant their only chance of meeting and enjoying a good gossip. The men pulled down the marquee and stored away the benches for another year, and restored everything to its usual order before the last family eventually departed.

" Where are the youngsters? " wondered Mrs. Brownley as the household turned towards the homestead. Amid the hustle and bustle of the sale and Black Diamond's disappearance, no one had noticed their absence.

"I thought they were playing with the other children," Bob said, "surely they wouldn't still be searching for Diamond?"

"Well, this will bring them," Mrs. Brownley grinned as she rang the bell loudly.

Popular opinion was that Diamond had escaped, and would return of her own accord, and, since it was well-nigh impossible to carry out a search among the hills and gullies in the gathering dusk, the best thing seemed to be to wait till morning

"The youngsters should be here soon," Bob remarked as he laid the tea-table, "they'd come as soon as they heard the bell." As if in answer to his words, hurried footsteps were heard outside. The family rushed the door, and opening it, cried in unison, "Have you found her?"

Margaret, a little ahead of Frank, looked at her young brother and then at the family, and said briefly, "We took Diamond away so she wouldn't be sold!"

The silence following her words was almost electric. Through Mrs. Brownley's brain coursed a relay of thoughts. The youngsters could have been acting out of sheer wilful disobedience; but they must have known they would be severely punished; no, the fact was that they were prepared to take any punishment for the sake of Jean's happiness— it was an evidence of unselfishness that she was glad to see in her children. Should they be punished? They had broken an unwritten law of the country; but, as Mrs. Brownley came to believe, they had been used of God to answer prayer. She felt it would be going against God to punish them.

A look that held much meaning passed between herself and her husband. To Margaret and Frank, the silence was more terrifying than any formidable sentence of punishment. The little group remained stationary, eyeing each other until Jean broke down in her mother's arms.

The anxious waiting of the past months, the strain of

that terrible day, and the final assurance that Diamond was still there, brought relief as she sobbed.

The others tactfully withdrew until Jean had composed herself. As soon as she recovered, the girl ran outside to make sure that Diamond was really there—the same, dear old Diamond, loving, beautiful, safe and sound !

" Diamond, old girl, you're mine still—perhaps for always ! " she murmured happily as she stroked the ebony neck.

And in all her joy, Jean did not forget the One Who had guided in everything, and her heart lifted in a prayer of loving gratitude, " O God, I can never thank You enough, but . . . please use me always to bring honour to Thy Name."

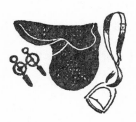

15

" OH, my! I'm tired of geometry! "

Jean opened her text-book one fine morning a few days after the sales. Her happiness was indescribable, as can be imagined, but more and more the feeling grew within her that Black Diamond was meant for some specific purpose.

Why had she seen the brumbies, and fallen in love with the black mare? Why was Diamond exceptionally good at jumping? Why had Diamond been used to save her life on that windy day when the falling branch had so nearly missed the two? Why had she helped to save the cattle from a fiery death in that glorious gallop down the mountain? Black Diamond was no ordinary horse; she had entered Jean's life for some good reason, but for what reason? It was very puzzling to Jean.

She sharpened a pencil and wrote " Geometry " in neat letters. " What's the date? " she wondered, and consulted a small calendar, exclaiming, " My hat! It's the 10th, and my birthday's on the 18th! I'd forgotten all about it ! "

The others, however, had not forgotten, and were sparing no effort to make the day a happy one.

The total income from the sales had risen to an amount that more than restored the needed money, and more than once Mr. and Mrs. Brownley had considered Bob's desire to be a missionary doctor ; but always they found that his training would cost more than they could yet afford.

" Perhaps next year, son," Mr. Brownley encouraged the boy, " we'll go easy this year, and save all we can for you."

" Gee, thanks a lot, Dad," Bob replied gratefully. He was still not sure how his parents had got to know of his ambition, but now that they were in the secret, he enjoyed discussing it with them.

Secret preparations for the birthday kept the Brownleys busy. Bob, Margaret, and Frank painted cards for the presents, while Mrs. Brownley, the family poet, racked her brain until she had produced some suitable verses to go with the cards.

The writing of poetry for Christmas and birthdays was an old family custom ; at such times, Mrs. Brownley, helped (or hindered) by her family, would compose some lines, usually very humorous, and would declare that she had done so for the last time ; but always on the next occasion she would forget her resolution, and set to the task once more.

The Brownleys knew how to keep a secret, being much practised in the art, so that Jean was quite unaware of the details, though she knew that her family would be preparing some surprise for her.

Jean awoke the morning before her birthday to the sound of a series of dull thuds issuing from the verandah outside. She glanced out to see the youngsters, clad in pyjamas, punching a fat pillow, suspended from a rafter, with energy and vigour that threatened the safety of the pillow-case.

" Hey, you kids ! " she called. Margaret, having dealt the pillow a forceful blow, turned her head in surprise, and caught the impact of the punching bag as it swung back.

" Ow ! " she cried, her gravity contrasting with Frank's shout of unfeeling laughter.

" Go easy on the pillow ! " Jean called again through the open window.

" It's tough," Frank calmly reassured her, " we've been punching it for nearly half-an-hour, and it hasn't tore yet ! "

" It hasn't torn ! " Jean corrected, in a shocked voice.

" Well, what are you worrying about? " grinned Margaret aptly. Jean couldn't help laughing.

" Anyway," she continued, " you'd better leave off now and do some work for your living."

The youngsters chuckled gleefully as they scampered inside to dress.

" I wonder what I'll get for my birthday? " thought Jean as she brushed her hair. The previous Sunday, her friends had given her their gifts—a dog brooch, a set of tube-paints, a packet of air-mail stamps (Jean was an enthusiastic philatelist), a cricket ball, and the many inevitable handkerchiefs.

" I get hankies every time," the girl had remarked at home, " I wish they'd think of something else."

" Would you rather have soap? " Mrs. Brownley had chuckled, and she had replied, " Well, at least you can use that up, but handkerchiefs just accumulate! "

Jean tried to forget about her birthday, but found she was too excited to do so. The atmosphere was full of suppressed excitement, and she deliberately avoided looking in nooks or crannies for fear of discovering hidden presents.

Mrs. Brownley had some important work to do in the kitchen, so after dinner she tactfully suggested to her daughter that the stock was due for another " once over ", and her daughter took the hint and tactfully offered her services.

She caught Diamond and rode her bareback to the summit of the Swagman, where she scanned the countryside for any trace of the stock, but found none.

" Well, Diamond, old lady, we've got our work cut out to find the herds, but I s'pose there's plenty of time."

Jean pressed her heels gently into the horse's flanks, but

Diamond refused to budge. " Go on, girlie ! " urged Jean, but still the mare stood her ground, frightened and restless.

" Go on, Diamond ! What's up? " And then the girl saw the cause of the trouble : a long black snake was gliding smoothly from under a rotten log.

Dismounting quickly, Jean picked up a nearby stick and brought it down heavily on to the snake. The long black form writhed in momentary agony, its back broken neatly. With the end of her stick, Jean threw it off the track, and continued on her way, for killing snakes was almost daily routine.

After a long search they found the cattle not far from Bungoola Peak, all in good condition, and then continued the hunt for the horses.

These they came upon in a clearing farther out, and Jean was fully satisfied with their appearance.

" I guess it's time we went home, Diamond," she murmured knowingly. They trotted downwards and reached the lower hills. Jean leaned forward and shortened the reins, and Diamond broke into a canter.

" Faster, lady ! " encouraged Jean. The mare responded eagerly, lengthening her stride as she thundered towards the creek. She cleared the water and galloped easily across the paddocks, jumping the fences until she had reached the horse paddock.

Jean slid off and patted the mare affectionately. " You little beauty, Diamond ! " she murmured, " you improve every minute ! " Diamond pricked her ears and nuzzled her mistress. She was happier now because the girl she loved was always gay, and the horse sensed that whatever had troubled Jean before and had sometimes made her sad, had been banished.

Jean entered the bungalow to find her mother reading peacefully on the shady verandah, and from her placid attitude, no one would have guessed that a quarter of an hour before Mrs. Brownley, with red face and anxious heart, had been working furiously for her daughter's happiness.

Next morning, Jean woke with a slight sense of foreboding —she did not like the thought of being sixteen, for, as she sometimes said, " I don't want to grow up—adults don't seem to have half as much fun ! "

After the milking, Jean came in to a delicious breakfast of steak and eggs, followed by bread and cream, and fresh, health-giving milk. The family ate hungrily until the once-laden table looked rather forlorn.

Mrs. Brownley cleared the empty dishes away, and Nob brought in a tray piled high with mysterious, exciting parcels. Under cover of the rustle, Frank whispered surreptitiously, " Don't forget the ' For she ' ! "

" What ' For she '? "

" For she's a jolly good fellow ! "

The family, grinning delightedly from ear to ear, stood up and sang a lusty version of that popular birthday song.

This completed, Jean unwrapped her first present—something bulky and smelling excitingly of leather. Jean cast aside paper and string to find . . . a shining, polished saddle !

" Oh ! " she shrieked, and sprang up to give her parents a bear-hug. Eventually, they emerged—safely—and Mr. Brownley laughed, " You don't know it's from us yet ! "

Jean returned to her place and picked up a beautifully painted card—Bob's handiwork. On the front page was a picture of Black Diamond jumping a fence, superscribed with the gold-painted words, " Loving Birthday Wishes ", and inside, a poem was decorated with a picture of the saddle. Jean read the poem, which ran thus :

> Though Jean loves Diamond an awful lot
> Her joy is incomplete.
> There's one thing that she hasn't got—
> She wants a better seat.
>
> So we have talked it o'er, and thought,
> " A good idea ! " said we.
> A nice new saddle we have bought
> To fill our girl with glee.

"Oh, Mummy, darling! Your style is unique!" chuckled Jean as she untied the second parcel. This, too, smelt of leather, and proved to Jean's supreme delight to be a gleaming bridle—from Margaret.

The next gift was Bob's contribution—a beautifully bound book of horse pictures that caused Jean to gasp as she turned the pages. All types, all colours, all sizes were painted beautifully by various prominent artists.

Underneath, a flat parcel was found to contain a very amateur-looking painting depicting a bush scene with a band of wild horses stampeding. Frank wriggled on his chair and offered explanation. "I couldn't think what you'd like, so I did that myself."

Jean saw ample proof of this as she regarded the picture: the horses were proportioned at random, and the trees reminded her of the Leaning Tower of Pisa, while here and there, small blotches and rubbings adorned the landscape. And as she looked, she thought of the loving care and patience, hard work and long hours, that had gone into the making of this gift, and vowed that she would keep it always hanging in a position of honour above her bed.

There was one more present: the men had clubbed together and bought a novel which promised to be a "thriller". At the end, were a number of telegrams and letters sent from relatives and friends.

Jean sighed a great sigh of contentment as she pushed back her chair. "Be off with you!" her mother cried as she waved a dish mop. "No wiping-up for the birthday girl!"

"Thank you, darling!" Jean replied, "I'll try out the new bridle and saddle." She ran off, her lessons forgotten, for it was the usual thing for the children to be relieved of their studies on such occasions.

Approaching the horse paddock, Jean whistled Black Diamond, and the mare trotted readily towards her. "We've got some new gear, old lady," the girl said as she slipped the bridle over Diamond's head, and put the saddle into position.

Diamond was curious ; these were both different from the usual harness—that she could tell by the smell—but they fitted better and were more comfortable.

Jean mounted, and they passed through the gate and towards the bungalow. The family came out to admire the effect ; Black Diamond looked more beautiful than ever now that the old saddlery had been replaced by the new.

" Let's take a photo," suggested Frank, and Bob ran inside for his camera.

Jean sat proudly, and Diamond stood erect, her head held high as if she knew that the picture they made would be recorded. But with all her cleverness, she could not know that in the near future her photos would appear far beyond the rural district where her home was.

" We'll go for a ride now, and try out the bridle and saddle," and with these words Jean wheeled her mount and cantered towards the gate, returning with a look of sheer joy on her face.

" It's lovely ! " she exclaimed, and galloped away again to the hurdle-paddock. The Brownleys watched her for a moment before turning to their work.

" Over we go, Diamond ! " urged Jean as she stood up in the stirrups to help the mare over a brush hurdle. They cantered up to the highest jump, and Diamond took it well.

" That's the spirit, girlie ! " Jean's voice grew contemplative. " I think it's a shame that hardly anyone knows you can jump—fewer still have seen you jumping, and they have to see it to appreciate it properly."

They rode for over half the morning, and then Jean returned to look through the book of horse-paintings.

" I must paint all these," she decided as she turned page after page. She came to the last plate and exclaimed, " Gee ! This is just like Diamond ! " The painting called " Lady and Lad " depicted a black mare with a white star and socks, her neck stretched protectingly over a dark grey foal.

After dinner, Jean read some of her new book, and started to paint with her new paints. Somewhat naturally, the picture she chose to copy was " Lady and Lad ", and by tea-time she had reproduced the painting well.

The evening meal included delicious strawberries and cream, jelly, cake and sweets.

In the waning light the family and the hands gathered on the front verandah for some games. When they had settled, Mr. Brownley said, " Now, for our first game, each person must write a question and answer on two strips of paper. These will be mixed up in two hats and read at random."

The party wrote busily, chuckling now and again. The questions and answers were then pooled, and Mr. Brownley and Bob chose them from two hats.

" What would happen if I cooked the dinner? " read Mr. Brownley.

Bob replied, " The horse would stampede ! "

" What would I do if the house blew up? "

" We'd all wash our nightshirts ! "

" What would happen if I lost my chewing-gum? "

" I'd shorten my braces ! "

" What would happen if Charger did a somersault? "

" We'd go to Mr. Stuart's for tea ! "

" What would we do if we spilt our porridge? "

" I'd suspect the box of gelignite ! "

" Oh dear, oh dear ! "—Mrs. Brownley was nearly convulsed, and the others were doubled up with laughter.

" We'd awaken the dead with our noise ! " remarked Mr. Brownley.

" More likely with the box of gelignite," Bob grinned quickly, " and if I cooked the dinner, they'd die again of poisoning ! "

" Now, for our next game," Mr. Brownley continued, " we each take a sheet of newspaper—and, oh ! wait a moment ! I've forgotten something." He dashed inside, and Jean started to read her sheet.

A heading attracted her attention, " Sydney Show to be held late this year." She looked up quickly.

" Mother, I'd nearly forgotten the Show . . . how could

I?" Her father came out, and Jean went on, "Dad, what about Diamond? She could make a name for herself in the jumps! Oh! I always knew she was meant for something!

"Yes, indeed! We'll have to start preparations immediately—we haven't much time, have we?"

Jean consulted the newspaper and answered, "It's to be held about half-way through April—gee! only a few weeks! We'll have to fly!"

The Brownleys always competed in the annual Sydney Show, and were well-established and widely known to be successful both in exhibits and events.

Frank, thinking of the promised excitement, danced with glee as he cried, "Yippee! Behold us making ourselves famous again at the Show! Whoopee! It's going to be fun!"

16

"THERE, Diamond! Nice girl! Now we're ready!"
Jean swung herself into the saddle and cantered
behind her father in the hot afternoon sunlight. They
were joined by Bob, Margaret, and Frank, and proceeded
up the slopes to where the herd of breeding cows were
looking after their young. These had to be brought in for
inspection, and the best primed for the Show, together with
the bull that was kept separately in a paddock.

"I think they'll be somewhere near the Peak, or the top
of the Swagman—the cool weather hasn't come yet," Mr.
Brownley remarked as they jumped the stream and pounded
over dry grass.

They found the herd, an hour later, grazing peacefully
half-way down Bungoola Peak, and with some little difficulty,
succeeded in piloting them towards the home paddocks.

The calves, averaging in age about five or six months,
frisked and gambolled beside their slower mothers, or
pranced ahead in a frolicking, jostling crowd.

Eventually, the animals were safely interned in a large paddock adjacent to the hurdle paddock.

" Whew ! " Mr. Brownley whistled as he surveyed them. " Only six weeks before we have to leave ! And in that time, we must prepare the horses, cattle, dogs, and fowls. And there's the fruit, and vegetables, and preserves—beside Mother's needlework and the children's art ! Shall we ever get through it all? "

" Oh, I guess so, Dad," Bob reassured, " we always do."

" We certainly will have our work cut out, though," Jean said. " Oh, boy ! Won't it be fun? "

" Are you going to pick out the best now, dear? " asked Mrs. Brownley, who had joined them.

" Yes—but it's going to be hard—they are all good enough to enter. I wish we could enter them all." Mr. Brownley considered. " Those four old ones can go back, and Bridget's side has that scar from the barbed wire."

The company stood watching the cattle for some time, until finally, the best had been chosen.

" That makes four." Mrs. Brownley looked over her husband's shoulder and counted the names he had written in a notebook. " There's Flossy, Venus, Clover, and Hotspur. That's enough, and their calves are good, too."

" Now we'll have to separate them," sighed Mr. Brownley, " and it's not going to be easy." The children's eyes gleamed in anticipation as he gave his orders. Two of them drove the cows into a corner of the paddock, while Mr. Brownley and Bob separated the four and drove them into an adjoining paddock. After some hard work this was accomplished, and the rejected cows were freed.

The four were plentifully supplied with food and water, and the workers went to the kitchen in response to the tea bell.

" That's one job done," Mr. Brownley sighed his satisfaction.

" What are you going to do tomorrow, dear? " his wife asked as she served large helpings of apple pie.

" Well, I think we'd better get the horses in and pick out the best there.   Charger will be entered, of course."

" Do you think he'll be Champion Stallion again, Dad? " Frank asked eagerly.

" Well, I wouldn't be surprised if·he was, and yet . . . he isn't getting any younger, you know."

" Are you going to bring them in in the morning or afternoon, Dad? " Jean joined in, a little anxiously, for she could not bear the thought of missing the excitement.

Mr. Brownley's eyes twinkled as he answered, " It looks as if I'll have to work on the cows in the morning, and bring the horses in after dinner, so that my young wild-woman will be able to study uninterruptedly ! "

" Oh, gee ! Thanks, Dad," his ' wild-woman ' replied as she reached up to a shelf for the family Bible.

Next day, the children worked hard at their lessons, using every ounce of their concentration so that they could be finished early.

After dinner, Mr. Brownley, Bob, Jean, and the young-sters saddled well-trained horses and rode towards Mount Guardian, where the horses had last been seen.

A level, smooth field stretched invitingly before them, and Bob suggested, " Let's have a race to the creek ! "

" No, over the creek," added Jean, " and finish up at that big gum tree."

The youngsters lined up with Bob and Jean, and Mr. Brownley good-naturedly shouted " Go ! "

The four horses sprang forward and pounded over the turf. Black Diamond naturally took up the front position, and reached the creek six yards ahead of the others. She hurled herself into the air and, landing, galloped with amazing speed until she had passed the tree.

" Good old lady," Jean said lovingly as she patted the wet black neck, " you've done it again, my beauty."

She wheeled the mare to face Bob, Margaret, and Frank, who finished in almost a straight line.

Bob remarked, " Might have known Diamond would

have it all to herself ! " and Jean chuckled, " She's lovely, isn't she, Bob? "

The party skirted the Swagman and cantered through a narrow gully that led to Mount Guardian, where they saw the horses a little above Evergreen Valley.

Charger neighed loudly at their approach, and Mr. Brownley shouted, " Bring 'em in, Charger ! " From a short distance, they watched while the black stallion gathered his mares and foals, and headed them unerringly towards the homestead paddocks.

The party scattered behind the herd, thus assisting Charger with any stragglers.

" We'll never get home at this rate," remarked Mr. Brownley, tiring of the jog trot, " if we had more time, it wouldn't matter ; but we'd better push them on a bit."

He shouted to the stallion, who broke into a canter, and did not slacken until they reached the paddocks ; soon the herd was safely installed in a large enclosure.

" Now comes the hard part," sighed Bob, " choosing the best."

Mr. Brownley extracted a notebook from his pocket, and wrote " Charger " at the top of the page. " Bouncer's a certainty, as usual," he commented, " next to Ginger, she's the best mare I've owned."

" Oh, Dad," Jean burst out indignantly, " Diamond's the best mare alive ! "

" I said, ' the best mare I've *owned*,' " her father grinned drily, and Jean was appeased.

" Sooty is still in top form," added Mrs. Brownley, who had come outside so that she would not miss anything, " and Treacle has turned out a beauty. That's three."

" Firefly and Floss are too old, aren't they, Dad? " Margaret put in, " but we must have Silver." Thus they considered, and finally decided to add Bluebird to those already selected.

" We'll have time to sort them out if we hurry," Mr. Brownley said as he mounted his gelding and gave orders.

As with the cows, two drove the herd into a corner, while he and Bob separated the six and drove them back into an adjoining paddock. The hands could have done this work, but Mr. Brownley thought it advisable to let his children have all the training they could get.

By the time the tea bell rang, Charger and the five mares and foals were enjoying food and water in their paddock, and the remainder of the band had been turned into a large enclosure a little distance away.

That night, all slept the deep unbroken slumber that follows hard work in the open, and restores for the next day ; and in the morning, Mr. Brownley concentrated on training the saddle horses—about the biggest job that lay before them.

The Brownleys were entering for many ring events, including hunting, camp drafts, and others, and this meant a lot of work for both horses and men.

As soon as Jean had washed up after dinner, she dashed outside and saddled Black Diamond, who was to undergo intensive training, for her young mistress was determined that her charge should carry off the honours.

Before she could, reach the horse paddock, however, Mr. Brownley met her and mentioned the fact that the cattle needed inspection. " I'd like to get them ready first, so that we can concentrate on the horses," he said, " and I want your help, Jean."

So with a little reluctance, the girl abandoned Black Diamond for the cattle paddock.

The youngsters were busy finishing landscapes of the mountains. Margaret had chosen a pretty stretch of the creek, while Frank produced a likeness to Bungoola Peak, rising sharply from surrounding hills. They put the finishing touches to the paintings, and stored their paints away.

When her other task had been completed, Jean mounted and rode to the creek where an old brush hurdle had been erected. " Now for the water-jump, my hearty," she encouraged, and cantered Black Diamond to the hurdle.

The horse leapt into the air, clearing fence and water in one magnificent bound.

" Good girl," Jean's praise came from the saddle, " you'll clean up the whole field at the Show if you keep it up ! " She jumped the mare back over the creek, and repeated the performance, and by the time the tea bell rang, Jean could not have been more fully satisfied.

" Tomorrow morning," Mr. Brownley said at the table, " we'll turn the cattle out and practise for the camp draft. Is that all right for you, dear? " He looked at his wife, who nodded, " Yes, I've finished the jam and nearly all the preserves. I'll be out as soon as you're ready." For Mrs. Brownley was entering for the Ladies' Camp Draft— herding steers—with her daughter.

" We've got to polish up the cattle yet, and the horses, and the dogs, and the fowls ! Oh, what a job ! " Mrs. Brownley always said that when she felt flustered. " And there's a heap of other things, too."

" Yes, we'll have to go hard," Mr. Brownley said, "as a matter of fact, I think the children could help in the morning, now, instead of doing their lessons."

A yell of delight greeted these words. " Perhaps they could do as much as they can before breakfast," his wife suggested with a little smile, " they shouldn't neglect their lessons altogether." The three concerned showed a little disappointment, but were pleased at missing at least some of their study.

Next morning they woke early and studied hard when the milking was done, and by breakfast they had completed a good part of their lessons.

Through the morning hours the stationers worked on, mustering cattle and horses in practice for the camp drafts. Black Diamond, as Jean had expected, excelled at this, too, for she dodged, chased, wheeled, and twisted with the graceful ease that was part of her nature.

" That mare is a real champion," Mrs. Brownley remarked as they penned the cattle for the last time. " You're a lucky girl, Jean."

Now there was always some hard work to do, training the horses, priming other animals, and preparing vegetables, fruit, and other exhibits. Each day brought the Show nearer, and likewise added to the general excitement.

One morning, as Jean came into the horse paddock, a bright idea seized her mind. Why not enter Diamond for the Novelty Event? The mare, with her intelligent mind, was quick to learn tricks : perhaps she could revise those she had learnt for Christmas ! ' They're not enough,' Jean thought, ' I'll have to teach her a few more.'

All day she thought out the tricks she could teach Diamond, and on the next day she rose an hour earlier to commence yet another branch of the mare's training. First, she went through the Christmas tricks, and was given one more proof of Diamond's wonderful memory, for the mare had not forgotten a thing.

Jean did not teach her anything new that morning, but made little additions to the tricks, such as standing on Diamond's back when the mare was on the stump.

So the days passed, and as they passed the children's lessons passed into the background until they were entirely forgotten. Day by day, the stationers threw themselves into their duties with ever-increasing energy and excitement. Now there was only a week to go before the Brownley stationers must leave for Sydney, and frantic last-minute preparations were in full progress. The hands took it in turn to accompany the Brownleys to the Show to help the animals, and this year Joe Wood and Ron Smith were the fortunate ones.

Everyone had worked conscientiously, and the stock was quite up to the Brownleys' high standard. Household entries, such as jam, preserves, cakes, fruit and vegetables were most tempting, and the children's paintings and handcrafts were very well done. Roosters and hens were looking their best, likewise the cattle, and Ruffles, Barney and Scamp were quite up to standard. All the entered horses were in their prime, and those in events had been excellently trained.

Jean had worked patiently with Black Diamond, and her range of tricks had increased, not to mention her jumping, which, if possible, was improving each day.

Eventually, after much impatient waiting, the last day dawned ; final touches were added to the exhibits, and the trunks were packed. The stationers repaired to bed early, for they had to be up at half-past three next morning, but judging from the noise issuing from the boys' and girls' bedrooms, the younger members were far too excited to sleep.

17

"R-R-R-R-R-RING!"

Mr. Brownley sprang out of bed and turned off the alarm. In the darkness, he could only just make out the time to be half-past three. He kissed his wife, who had awakened, and went to call the others.

They needed no second bidding. One and all rose hastily, eager in their excitement, and were soon working hard.

A passenger train from Brisbane would be leaving Aruntoora at ten past eight, and the stock would be following some hours later in a small freight train.

"Isn't it time to go yet, Dad?" Frank asked impatiently as he stood ready.

"Nearly," his father smiled down at him, "we may as well leave soon—better be sure than sorry." For the Brownleys, always punctual, had completed their work and had time to spare.

Jean ran outside and said goodbye to Black Diamond; in this farewell there was no sorrow, but only excitement and hope, as Jean murmured to the mare, "We're going in the Show together, Diamond, you and I. God will help us, girlie, and we're going to be a great success, aren't we, my pet?"

Mrs. Brownley called, and Jean ran into the house,

collected her overcoat and a book, and with the others, crowded into the lorry and took her seat on a pile of portmanteaux.

" I just feel as if we'll never get there ! " Margaret sighed ; the patient waiting was, she felt, a load far too heavy for her young shoulders.

" Patience is a virtue, possess it if you can :

Seldom seen in woman, and never seen in man ! " chanted Jean, who was feeling as anxious herself.

They jolted downwards, with a bump and a bang and a jar, and rumbled heavily over the wooden bridge spanning the creek. In the early morning light, the truck wended its painful way down and along, while its occupants joked light-heartedly.

" Half-way ! " Frank sang joyously as they passed the half-way mark—a certain gnarled, twisted gum with an enormous growth on one side. On and on they drove while the sun mounted higher in the heavens, and at last, they reached the station.

Everyone helped to unload the truck, and soon all the portmanteaux were safely stored on the platform. Mr. Brownley had a friendly chat with the station-master, and then returned to give a few last-minute orders and words of advice to Clive Richardson, who was to drive the lorry back.

" Here's the train ! " cried Jean, who had been watching the line anxiously. The engine puffed into the station and came to a standstill, and the travellers, having put their heavier luggage in the guard's van, scrambled into the last carriage but one.

" Goodbye, Clive ! "

" Goodbye, everybody ! "

Last farewells were called as the train steamed out of the station, and commenced to chug steadily downwards.

The stationers, who occupied a whole section of the carriage, spread themselves comfortably and settled down to the twenty-hour journey.

The younger Brownley members were, however, far too

excited to settle, for train journeys—even the sight and smell of trains—spelt excitement to them, in brilliant letters.

At last they steamed into Central and pulled to a stop. The stationers alighted on to the platform, collected the luggage from the guard's van, and passed through the barrier to the busy area without, and stood in the midst of a crowd of people, refreshment bars, and luggage cars driven by girls who all but ran them over.

" The first thing now is breakfast," Mrs. Brownley said in her practical way, and with eagerness they made their way to the overcrowded restaurant.

When they had finished, they engaged a taxi from the rank just outside the station, and were driven to their usual boarding-house at Centennial Park, near the Showground.

" Well, well, and how are you all? " Mrs. Grant, the boarding-house keeper, greeted the travellers cheerily, as they filed into the hall.

" This is Joe Wood—Mrs. Grant." Mr. Brownley introduced the only member of the Brownley household with whom the lady was not familiar, before being shown the usual rooms.

That morning they did not do much ; Mr. Brownley, accompanied by his children, went over to the Showground and completed some of the official arrangements, and stayed to look over stock that had already arrived.

At three o'clock, Mr. Brownley, Joe, and Ron went to Flemington to collect their animals, which were due soon after four. Having engaged trucks, they returned to the Showground, and installed their stock comfortably before returning to their lodging.

As soon as the others knew their animals had arrived, they dashed over to greet them. Jean found Black Diamond instinctively, and threw her arms around the mare's thick neck, as she laughed excitedly, " Oh, Black Diamond, we're here at last ! Isn't it going to be fun? "

Diamond nosed her young mistress affectionately, for she had missed her even during the thirty-six hours.

That night the menfolk slept with the animals, for the stock was valuable and caution had to be taken.

Next morning all were up early, cleaning out the stalls and boxes by half-past six. Mr. Brownley had more business to do while the others exercised the stock.

Jean had entered Black Diamond for hunting, high-jumping, the novelty event, and others, and practice was resumed energetically. Diamond's form was unaffected by the travelling, and her young mistress was thrilled as she put her through her paces.

The Brownley's had a fairly large part to play in the Show, with their horses, cows, dogs and other exhibits. Joe and Ron were entering for buck-jumping and steer-riding: Jean had expressed a wish to join them, but her parents had flatly refused.

Daily more people and stock arrived, until the Show-ground became a hive of activity. Newspaper reporters ran round with cameras and notebooks, recording ' charming studies ' of various competitors, and flattering them immensely.

Jean was just taking Black Diamond to the first hurdle one day when she was snapped, and the photographer came up to ask for her name, remarking that she looked an excellent little horsewoman, and how nice she and Diamond looked together.

Day after day preparations went furiously ahead. The Brownleys also took time to look around at the others.

" We're going to have some keen competition this year," Mr. Brownley remarked, during one tour of inspection, " there are some fine beasts there."

" Ours are the best, though, I think," his wife put in proudly.

" They always are," Frank joined in, as though stating the obvious, " but sometimes the judges can't see straight, an' they get mixed up and put the prizes on the wrong ones ! "

The eight then went as a body to look at the shetland ponies.

" Aren't they lovely little things? " Mrs. Brownley was as fascinated as ever by the cheeky, toy-like ponies.

" I remember seeing this one in last year," Margaret remarked, " he's got a bad temper." She approached a young chestnut who laid his ears and snapped in response to her friendly overtures.

" You're nearly as bad as Jean when it comes to going for the wild 'uns, Margie," her young brother teased as they went on.

They passed boxes of goats and made their way through more sideshows towards the horse pavilions. They entered Pavilion A and inspected as closely as possible the horses that had already been assembled there.

" Nice lot of horses, this year," Ron remarked as they left the pavilion for B, where their horses were stalled. By this time, hunger pangs were urging the party homewards, so they abandoned the Showground and planned to visit a city church on the morrow.

The Show would open on the following Saturday, so all that week the competitors were working hard. Sometimes the horses would be exercised in Centennial Park, a favourite haunt of riders, to give them a change. Here there were no huge buildings, just acres of trees and grass, which seemed more like home to the horses, and put them more at their ease. Naturally, the stock longed for its accustomed freedom on the station, and became restless in the confinement of their stalls, so they were taken out as often as possible.

Black Diamond, especially, grew nervy, but with Jean to soothe her, and plenty of exercise, she kept her form well. Surrounded by an ever-increasing number of people, the mare learnt to become accustomed to a crowd—a valuable asset when competing in big shows.

Jean, taking her through her entire repertoire of tricks

one morning, felt yet another warm glow of satisfaction and pride, for Diamond was progressing rapidly. To the tricks she had learnt last Christmas, she had added jumping over a burning rail, walking on hind legs, dancing and carrying flags.

The highlight of all these Jean was perfecting now. The girl mounted her horse and rode her bareback around a small ring. Diamond, however, tripped and fell, and Jean rolled off on to the grass. The mare lowered her head, lifted her mistress in her strong teeth, and carried her to a small box. Here Diamond lay down, and Jean almost rolled on to her back. Diamond rose slowly, and the pair cantered off again.

" Well done, Diamond, my hearty," Jean praised the mare as she gathered her material and walked out of the arena with Diamond following faithfully, her head over Jean's shoulder. " It's not long now, girlie, before we'll be doing our stuff in front of thousands. Oh, boy ! It's going to be grand, isn't it, lass? "

Black Diamond snorted her answer softly in Jean's ear, as the pair wended their way to Horse Pavilion B.

" Hullo, Jean ! "—a tall thin girl in khaki jodhpurs greeted her as she unlocked the door of Diamond's stall and led her charge inside.

" Oh, hullo, Peggy. I've just been putting Diamond through her tricks. She learns quickly."

" Yes, I saw you on Saturday when you were practising. She certainly is a beaut little mare. Say ! Where did you get to on Sunday? I was looking for you everywhere. I thought we could try our horses out together. I'd like to get mine used to crowding."

Under her sun tan, Jean flushed a little as she replied, " We went to church in the morning and evening."

A slightly scornful look passed over Peggy Arnold's face as she returned with a careless laugh, " Church ! Oh, I wouldn't know much about that ! You should've bumped along with us. A whole crowd of us went for a picnic in the afternoon."

"Then I should *not* have gone with you!" Jean exclaimed emphatically, "if you can't spare God one day out of seven, surely you're being rather selfish!"

Peggy stood a little aghast at this speech. She tried to find a suitable answer, but failed, and decided to make a graceful exit.

Jean looked after her week-old friend and bit her lip. She felt very indignant, and wished she could have given proper vent to it. She did not know, however, that her few forceful words had given Peggy Arnold something to think about.

"I s'pose she'll tell everyone I'm a wowser," Jean thought. "Oh, well, I'm glad, anyway!" She rubbed Black Diamond down and made her comfortable before leaving to find Bob, who had left his exercise a short time before for a milk-shake.

From that day, Peggy's attitude towards Jean changed. The two girls, nearly the same age, had met often during practice, and, since Peggy's hack was stalled opposite Black Diamond, they had also seen a lot of each other in the pavilion. It had not taken them long to get to know each other, and a pleasant acquaintance had grown up between them. But Jean's few revealing words had shocked the sensitive Peggy: she had thought Jean would be what she called ' a decent sort ', and not a religious stick-in-the -mud. Yet Jean had proved to be pretty decent—perhaps it was only on Sundays that she was different.

But thinking back, Peggy realized that Jean's whole outlook was different—she was not impatient with the horses when they were nervy, she didn't swear when things went wrong, she never got ' down in the dumps '—always cheerful, kind, considerate, and nice. It was rather mysterious to Peggy, so she decided to watch Jean carefully, and find out a bit more if she could. The words, too, had given her food for thought. Up to that time, God had been to her merely Someone very far away, but Jean's speech had given her another aspect of God as the great Creator Who made some demands on her life.

'Oh, well, I'm too young to worry about it yet,' she thought to herself, and tried to push the matter to the back of her mind.

Day after day went by, and each day Peggy watched Jean closely, and became more mystified. One or twice she asked a question, seemingly carelessly, but with a longing for understanding, and Jean explained clearly and simply the Gospel and its meaning.

Peggy was still very doubtful, however, when Friday dawned. Activity was intensified everywhere, last-minute preparations were carried out, and one and all waited expectantly, excitedly, for the morrow, when the Show would begin.

18

"OH, boy!" Jean sat up in bed and gazed out of the attic window on to the street below. "Oh, boy!" she exclaimed again, "this is the day!" Although it was only just after five o'clock, she could not bear to laze any longer, and sprang out of bed. Dropping on her knees, she prayed an earnest prayer.

She had many things to pray and praise about, but uppermost in her mind this morning was a petition for success in the Show.

Dressing quickly, she crept downstairs to go for a walk in the solitude of the park.

"Gee, I'm excited!" Margaret exclaimed as she and Frank groomed their horses after breakfast. With the two elder children, and their father, the youngsters were to lead the competitors in the first day's events, and all were now working hard to give a sheen to the coats of the horses. This was not without its difficulties, however, for the stallion and the mares, leading a vigorous free life, were not accustomed to the amount of attention they now received.

At last, everything was ready. Mr. Brownley proudly led Charger through the crowded lane from the pavilion to the Marshalling Yard under the Martin and Angus grandstand, and after being checked, waited while the Show was officially opened.

The rest of the Brownley household was leaning excitedly on the rail near the grandstand, watching the splendid line of stallions that filed into the arena.

"Here comes Charger!" Bob cried as the black stallion, his coat shining beautifully, and his head held high, stepped lightly from the yard.

They could see Mr. Brownley giving the horse a final assuring pat as they followed the line to the judges' stand.

"Oh! I hope Charger is champion again," Mrs. Brownley murmured, "this will be the fifth time!"

At last, the nine stallions were lined up before the judge, and started to parade.

"Look at that sorrel!"

"That cream one's better!"

"I like the roan!"

"Isn't that black one a beauty?"

"That chestnut is out," Mrs. Brownley remarked as one of the thoroughbreds was rejected, "and there goes the grey!"

After much wearisome waiting, and pondering of the judges, two more horses were taken out. "Charger's still there!" breathed Frank, who had watched as eagerly as the others, "he'll be champion, for sure!"

The judges moved among the stallions, speculating, and after a while, they gave them their ribbons and placed them in order. A big-boned, fine-looking bay headed the line, followed by Charger! Three others almost as beautiful came next.

"Oh! Charger's only Reserve Champion!" Jean ejaculated, her face clouded with disappointment. Mrs. Brownley couldn't help laughing.

"Only Reserve Champion!" she echoed. "He's lucky to be that."

The winners began a small parade, and the four children dashed away to bring the mares which the hands had already assembled in the Marshalling Yard.

Amid band-music and applause from the surrounding grandstands, the stallions were led out, and the thoroughbred mares were led in, and paraded before the judges, showing off their paces.

One by one, the mares were rejected, until there were only five left, two of which were Bouncer and Treacle. The judge pondered for some little time, before placing the remainder in a line.

" Bouncer's Champion ! " Mr. Brownley grunted his satisfaction, and his wife, by his side, added, " And Treacle's got second prize ! "

Amid more applause, the thoroughbreds were led out, and the Brownleys greeted one another excitedly outside the Marshalling Yard.

" Gee ! Haven't we done well so far? " Margaret exclaimed, as they made their way to Horse Pavilion B.

" Our work's over for today, anyway," commented Mr. Brownley, " they're going to judge the Arabs and Trotters and the draught horses now. I'm thinking they'll have their hands full ! "

The next day was Sunday, and the stationers decided to attend the services in the same church.

Peggy Arnold watched Jean closely in the morning, when they were cleaning out the stalls : she was on the lookout for any " extra piety ", as she called it, but found none.

" What are you doing today, Jean? " she asked as care-lessly as she could.

" Going to church," was the firm reply.

" Poor you ! " Peggy murmured.

Jean swung round and looked at her companion steadily. " I often thank God," she said definitely, " that I have been brought up in a Christian home, and that I have been taught the value of the Christian life."

Peggy did not answer : she shrugged her shoulders and bent to her task. Watching Jean for the past few days, she had often had cause to think that perhaps there was something in all this business, after all. Jean certainly spoke as if she meant it, and she really was always happy and contented, even when things went wrong.

And then, suddenly, she decided on a bold move. " Jean," she said, her tone changed, " could I come to church with you, tonight? "

Jean's heart leapt. " Why ! Of course you can ! Bring the gang, if you like " (naming Peggy's friends).

" I don't think they'd come," the other answered wryly,

" but I'd like to come. I've got a couple of decent dresses somewhere here, and a hat. I'll dig them out this afternoon."

" All right, Peg, and I'll meet you just outside the main gate at half-past six. Is that all right? "

So Jean, having completed her work and made Diamond comfortable, ran off to tell her family the glad news, and Peggy, looking after her, murmured, " Now I'll find out just what all this is about."

That evening, as the Brownleys passed by the Showground entrance on their way to the tram, a figure, dressed and made up heavily, stepped out of the shadow and looked for Jean. The latter saw her quickly and took charge of her for the rest of the evening.

At church the minister spoke of God's love, how He had sent His Son to give His life for us, and how ungrateful we are if we do not give Him our lives in return, and also how foolish we are when we choose Eternal Death rather than Eternal Life.

Peggy sat through the service as if spellbound. The words seemed to take hold of her, and sank deep into her heart.

That night, she could not sleep. Through her mind, the words kept repeating—" Eternal Life . . . or Eternal Death . . . Eternal Life . . . or Eternal Death." Miserably, she knew that she did not merit an ounce of God's mercy. Suppose she died . . . tonight ; what would happen to her? From the words she had heard in church, she knew there was only judgment ahead for her.

But it meant giving up everything she liked. What would the gang say? They'd say she was a fool, too young to worry about such stuff. No ! She couldn't do it ! She'd think about it later, when the Show was over, and not worry her head about it yet.

But Peggy was to find that she could not put such a matter in the background. Moment by moment, it kept troubling her, so that she knew no peace.

The next day was given over to the judging of ponies,

saddle ponies and harness ponies, and as all the children had been taught to handle big-boned hunters as soon as they could sit a horse, the Brownleys did not possess any ponies, and an easy day stretched before them.

They had not had much success with the other stock this year. Their bull gained a third prize, and Scamp a second prize, but the Brownleys were not too disappointed, as their first concern was with the horses.

So Monday gave place to Tuesday, when saddle- and harness-horses were to be judged. Jean was entering Black Diamond for the class for saddle-horses, and hoped for good results, for everywhere she had met people who praised the black mare loudly.

The other saddle-horses belonging to the Brownleys were also entering for various contests, and so the day promised to be a busy one. Diamond was entered for two classes for horses who had not previously won a prize at the Sydney Show ; Mrs. Brownley and Jean were to ride in a Ladies' Hack class ; and Mr. Brownley and Bob were entered in a Gentlemen's Hack class.

Jean was on first, so promptly at a quarter to nine she took the mare, groomed immaculately and more beautiful than ever, to the Marshalling Yard. After anxious moments of waiting, the great door slid open, and the line of saddle-horses in the first competition paced slowly out.

" Yoohoo, Jean ! " Frank cooed from the rails, and Jean turned her head quickly for a brief grin to her family.

" I've got some stiff opposition," she thought as she paraded Diamond with the other horses. Her thoughts were justified, too, for the hacks were really magnificent.

Jean found it unnecessary to hold Diamond's head up, for the mare, although excited by the crowds, seemed to grasp the situation, and was showing off beautifully.

At last, they came to a halt in a long line before the judge, who considered for some time, and, at intervals, rejected one of the competitors. Jean's heart sank into her boots every time he came her way, but always he passed her.

Eventually, there were only three left—and Diamond was one of them. The judge came up and placed them in order—a blue-grey, a chestnut, and the black mare!

With her heart singing, Jean followed the first two hacks out of the ring. Diamond third! In her first contest!

Outside, she was greeted excitedly by the Brownleys and the two hands, who crowded round and praised the mare enthusiastically.

There was a class for galloways next, and then Jean was on again, so she waited in the Marshalling Yard while the next competition was carried out. As the entrants for the next class arrived, Jean glanced over them and noted that they were practically the same as in the first class, but . . . the two horses that had beaten Diamond were not there!

' There are others just as good though,' the girl thought gloomily, and immediately chided herself. Hadn't she prayed for success for a long time? Wasn't the prize money important for a very special, secret reason? If it was God's will, Diamond would be successful.

The second contest was over. The door opened again, and the third class sallied forth. As before, Diamond could have been a show veteran in her behaviour, as they paraded and then stood still. As before, Jean's heart sank whenever the judge came near her, but she was still there when there were only three left!

With bated breath she waited while the judge considered. Finally, he came up and led Diamond to first place.

With thankful pride Jean led the others off the field. Diamond stepped higher than ever, and Jean sat tall and straight. This was a moment of moments.

Once outside, the triumphant pair were surrounded again by the Brownleys. Peggy Arnold, who had watched as eagerly as the others, came up with her congratulations.

There was another galloway class, and then Diamond, to Jean's immense delight, won another Ladies' Hack class, before her father competed successfully in a Gentle-men's Hack contest.

The Brownleys hugged themselves with glee at their success. " It won't be long now," Mr. Brownley said as they wended their way to a café, " before we'll be in the ring events, and *then* we'll see what we can do ! "

19

"YIPPEE! Diamond, it's going to be great!" Jean joyfully told the mare as she groomed her on Wednesday morning.

That day the jumping and trotting exhibitions were to begin, and the two were competing in two hunting events in the afternoon.

Amid festive band music the Show started, and Mr. Brownley, riding Warrior, the station's second-best hunter, tied for second in a gentlemen's hack class. But in the next event, Warrior's left foreleg was injured by a fractious sorrel, and he became too lame to run until three days later.

"That rules poor old Warrior out of the other things," Bob mourned, "Goodbye, I'm on soon."

Sometime later, Mrs. Brownley and Jean rode out to compete in a ladies' hunting class. Riding Peter with the poise of a born horsewoman, Mrs. Brownley completed the course, and it was Jean's turn.

"Come on, Diamond," the girl encouraged, for the mare, excited and frightened by the noisy Show-ring, had become more and more restive. "Girlie, come on, steady now," Jean soothed desperately, for in response to a flick of the reins, the mare merely described a circle near the judge's box.

And then, an "S O S" to her Heavenly Father, and excellent horsemanship combined to get the upper hand, and Diamond, springing forward under a smart whack on the rump, approached the first hurdle, and cleared it neatly. The crowd gave vent to a murmur of applause, for even in her nervousness, the mare had not forgotten how to jump.

" Good girl," Jean encouraged, cheerful again, as Diamond cantered more readily up to the second hurdle. With growing confidence, she poured herself over the third like a smooth stream of water, and a roar of appreciation echoed from stand to stand.

That roar proved fatal, however, for Diamond, thoroughly startled by the noise, baulked at the next fence, and dislodged her rider, thereby losing all chance of a prize.

Outside, Jean was greeted with condolences from her family, who crowded round and offered praise to Mrs. Brownley, who had gained third place, and hope for better things for Diamond.

Jean, surprisingly, was not very disappointed about the failure ; she knew that God had answered her prayer, and had shown the crowds Diamond's ability, but He had had to refuse her a prize to teach her how to bear disappointment, and Jean knew that all things, good or bad, " work together for good to them that love God."

The next event was the first of two harder hunting-jumping contests, for which Diamond was entered. Both were tests for the best horses, who were to be tried over courses comprised of gates, hurdles, wall, and so on.

" We're praying for you," Mrs. Brownley smiled as Jean rode into the Marshalling Yard.

" Thanks, Mummy, I'll be needing it," she replied, for Diamond was still troublesome. Jean herself was praying hard, for these were very important events, and the girl felt confident that Diamond would be successful if she overcame her nervousness. She talked to the mare while waiting her turn, and Diamond was quieter and more easy as she trotted on to the field.

With another prayer in her heart, Jean cantered up to the first obstacle, the log. Under Jean's familiar, assuring touch, the mare took less notice of the crowds this time, and pricked her ears as she gently, easily took the jump.

A murmur from the crowd greeted this act, and Jean urged her on a little to the picket. This was overcome in the effortless way peculiar to born hunters, and Diamond swung round a tricky corner and over the rails. Another turn, and over a three-foot platform, and there was a little stretch before them.

" Come on, Diamond, old lady," Jean encouraged, for the jumps were harder now, and many horses had lost their chances here. Diamond increased her speed a little, gathered herself gently, and sailed gracefully over the gate.

The murmur was louder this time, but it failed to disturb the mare, who had settled down to enjoy the sport she loved. Up and over the wall she soared, more assured now, and turned to take the rails.

She needed no urging as she swept over two more jumps, and Jean rode off the field amid a storm of applause.

" That was marvellous, Jean ! " Mr. Brownley congratulated as his daughter slid to the ground. " I knew you'd be all right, because we were praying for you."

" Yes, Dad," Jean grinned happily, " I was praying, too, and Diamond didn't give an ounce of trouble. Isn't it great, having a Father like ours? "

And God had indeed said " Yes " this time, for a little while later it was announced that Black Diamond was the easy winner !

The Brownleys could not compete in hunting in pairs or fours contests, owing to Warrior's injury, but next day Mrs. Brownley and Jean went in an Equestrienne Jumping Contest, which Jean won.

Now there were some trotting events, so the Brownleys

had time to relax.   Bob and Jean watched an exciting race,
and then made their way to the horse pavilion to join the
others.

Approaching the pavilion they saw a harnessed trotter,
who was giving her jockey some trouble.   The man was
holding him well, but a passer-by knocked the whip out of
his hand, and as he stooped to pick it up, the horse, with
a sudden mighty twist of his head, broke loose and plunged
madly through the crowd, scattering people in his path.

A woman screamed and snatched her child just in time,
as, with frightened people falling back on either side, the
trotter careered madly along the lane.

Bob saw him coming straight towards them, and dashed
right in front of him.   The trotter reared high and nearly
shattered his carriage, but as he came down, he dodged to
the left, and would have gone on, had not Jean been too
quick for him.   With a mighty effort, she grabbed the
bridle and hung on desperately while the foaming horse
side-stepped in an attempt to free himself.   Bob came up,
and held the bridle, and Jean took a hand off to stroke the
glistening neck.

" There now, boy !   What's all this fuss about, eh? " she
crooned.   " What's the matter, old fellow? "

Jean's power over animals, always so effective, had
ample opportunity now.   The frightened, bewildered
trotter ceased to fret and stamp, and stood quietly, panting,
while the jockey came running up and gratefully took
charge.

From out of the crowd that had gathered, a reporter
approached, and Jean gasped as she recognized his movie-
camera.   " Just took a shot of that," he grinned at the
brother and sister.   " May I have your names, please? "

" Is this for a newsreel?"   Bob stared a little.

" Yes, and I'm sure it's something to be proud of."

" Oh, that's all right.   Come on, Jean."

" Wait a moment."   Another reporter stepped up and
said, " Aren't you the lass that owns the black mare?   Your
name is Jean Brownley, isn't it? "

Jean smiled a little ruefully, and replied, "Yes, and my brother, Bob." The two men grinned and wrote something down, while the pair made a hasty retreat from all this confusing publicity.

"Whew!" Bob whistled, "I hope that doesn't happen too often!"

His sister laughed and went off to saddle Diamond for the next water-jumping class.

Diamond, though good at any sort of jumping, did not stand out in long jumps as in high jumps, so she failed to secure a place in the first one, though she gained a third prize in the second.

The next day, Friday, passed by as the others: Diamond competed in two more water-jumps, but without success.

On Saturday, many of the high jumps were carried out. Jean had entered Diamond for the Ladies' High Jump, but not for any of the others for she knew that Diamond would not do so well with a strange rider.

"I wish I could masquerade as a boy," she said gloomily to Bob, "I think it's mad not letting women ride in all the high jumps!" Jean watched the jumping carefully, and wondered if Diamond could beat any of the winners . . . she was soon to find out.

Just after lunch, Jean rode Diamond into the arena for the second hunting-jumping contest, even harder than the first one.

With a prayer in her heart and encouraging words on her lips, she cantered the mare up to the brush hurdle, three and a half feet high, and Diamond easily overcame it. They went on to the rails, gates, wall, and picket, each jump two inches higher than the last, and swung round for the two six-and-a-half feet poles. Collected and lithe, Diamond flew over them, and was ushered out amid a storm of applause, for the experienced people could tell that the mare would win, even before it was announced.

"What's wrong, Jean?" Mrs. Brownley asked, as the Brownleys ate a sumptuous tea some time later.

"Diamond's on tonight, in the high jump," was the

somewhat agitated reply, " I hope she won't be scared of the floodlights."

Her father laughed. " She'll be all right, Jeanie," he smiled, " and if she couldn't beat the last winning jump, of six foot nine, I'll eat my hat ! "

" Will you really, Dad? " Frank leaned forward and opened two brown eyes very wide.

" Of course not," Bob retorted, " because Diamond's going to beat six foot nine, and clean up the whole field ! "

Soon after tea, Jean saddled Black Diamond and waited, ready for her turn. An open high jump was completed, the winner clearing six foot eleven, and then some trotting races were run.

" It's getting late," Margaret remarked, " isn't it time for your class, Jean? "

" Ought to be starting in ten minutes' time," her sister muttered anxiously, " and there's another two races yet."

Suddenly a hollow voice boomed over the amplifiers, announcing that owing to a delay some of the events, including the Ladies' High Jump, would have to be run off on the morrow. The Brownleys turned horrified faces to each other.

" Sunday ! " Mr. Brownley uttered. " Oh, Jeanie I'm afraid that rules you out of the High Jump ! "

Jean clenched her hands . . . she had been waiting and hoping eagerly for this event. " Yes, of course, Dad," she choked.

" I think that's positively wicked ! " Bob exploded, partly in sympathy, but mostly from conviction.

" I shouldn't wonder if the churches had something to say about that," Mrs. Brownley put in, " even the Show is used now to rob us of the Lord's Day ! "

In bed that night Jean tried hard to conquer her rebellion. She pounded the pillow with her fists, and wished dismally that she could dress up as a boy and enter for one of the other high jumps.

And then she realized that she was fighting in her own

puny strength, instead of handing the matter over to the Stronger than the strong.

" O God," she prayed, " please forgive me, and help me now. And if it's Thy will, do overrule about the high jump—I know You can—but, O God, Thy will be done! "

Then Jean pulled the bedclothes closer around her, and fell asleep.

Early next morning, as Jean was cleaning out Diamond's stall, Peggy came up with a little smirk on her face. " Well, Jean, I s'pose you're staying here for the high jump, aren't you? "

Jean straightened. " Oh, no," she said, " I'm going to church."

Peggy gave a little derisive laugh. " I s'pose you prayed about this, didn't you, *saint* Jean? And now what's going to happen? Doesn't look as if you're going to get an answer this time, does it? "

" Peggy," the other replied calmly, " God always answers the prayers of His children, but sometimes He has to say ' No ' to us, so that we can be taught a lesson that is all for our good. Naturally, I have prayed about the high jump, and I believe that, if it's God's will, Diamond will go in for it, and win. But I have to be willing for Him to refuse, in His great kindness, if it is better that way."

Peggy eyed the speaker soberly : she was dumbfounded with something approaching admiration for her friend. " Oh, well," she remarked aimlessly, and turned to go, but just as her hand was on the door, the girls heard a patter on the roof, increasing rapidly until it became a heavy drumming.

" Gee ! hailstones ! " Peggy muttered, " what a storm ! " The two stayed marooned in the pavilion for more than an hour, and then suddenly an amplified voice was heard above the noise of the pavilion and clatter of the rain.

" Owing to the exceedingly unfavourable weather," it droned, " the events that were to be run off today are postponed again until the ground is suitable. We hope that will be tomorrow."

Jean looked at Peggy. Peggy looked at Jean. " Oh, Jean," was all she said. Jean smiled and murmured a fervent, " Thank You, God ! "

The Brownleys attended the same church morning and evening, and Peggy went with them. At night, she listened attentively to the good news of a Saviour for sinful lives, and again she was challenged, so that then and there she yielded herself to Christ, so that He might give His Life to her ; and this, she declared, was the greatest event of all her life.

Monday dawned, the last day of the Show, and Jean woke with rather mixed feelings. The high jump was on that day—the most important event to her ; and she couldn't help wondering if Diamond was really good enough. Then, all this excitement was nearing its end, and soon they would be leaving the crowded, noisy city for the peace and quiet of the calm mountains once more. Jean was not sorry, however, for she had had her annual fill of urban excitement.

Just after ten o'clock she took Diamond to the Marshalling Yard, and waited with about twenty other entrants. She knew all her family were praying for her, and her faith in her Heavenly Father gave her the confidence she needed as she rode on to the field.

Three horses took the five-foot-six jump, and it was Diamond's turn. Jean leaned forward a little and cantered the mare towards the rails. She felt a gentle gathering of the lithe body as Diamond took off and landed with her customary ease and grace.

The others took their turn, and then the rail was raised to six feet. Diamond cleared the jump with scarcely more effort than she had used for the first.

Now the rail was to be raised at the discretion of the Stewards, and each horse was allowed three attempts. The first horse failed, but Diamond was as competent as ever.

Little by little, the rail was raised, and the number of horses decreased as steadily, until only six were left. The height was six-and-a-half feet now, and Jean was conscious of just a little tautening of the muscles as the mare leapt over it.

The height went up, and finally only three horses were left. Now the winner was to be chosen, and the crowds in the grandstands stirred expectantly.

Eventually it was a contest between a bay gelding and the black mare.

" I told you Diamond could beat six foot nine," Bob remarked as the height was raised to six feet ten. His young sister smiled.

" Now you won't have to eat your hat, will you, Daddy? " she laughed.

" That bay is good stuff," Frank muttered. " Looks as if Jeanie is going to have some tough opposition ! "

The bay was certainly hard to beat. At seven feet one he faltered, however, and Diamond was left victorious.

" Hurrah ! Diamond's won ! " The youngsters shouted themselves hoarse in their glee.

" What's happening now? " Mr. Brownley screwed up his eyes as he watched Jean talking to the judge, and then guiding the black mare back to the run. " My hat ! " he exclaimed, " she's going to try for it ! "

" What? Not the record? " his wife cried.

But there was no time for the answer, for the judge's voice was coming over the microphone. " Ladies and gentlemen," he said, " Miss Brownley has decided to try to beat the Royal Sydney Record, which stands at seven foot six, on her mare, Black Diamond."

The Brownleys gasped and looked at each other with mixed expressions of excitement and fear. " Oh, I hope she does ! " Bob exclaimed fervently.

The rail was raised to seven foot four and five, but Diamond seemed unperturbed. Seven foot six, and Jean tried hard to control her feelings and encourage the mare. She leapt over it, and the rail was raised another inch.

" Oh, Diamond, you must do this. You must. O Father, *please* help us ! " Jean breathed.

Diamond cantered quickly up to the jump, and soared

into the air like a mighty bird. Jean stood up in the stirrups, and leaned back as the mare landed, and a peal of applause thundered from stand to stand.

" Oh ! She's done it ! " Mrs. Brownley clasped her hands.

" Jean can't leave the judge alone ! " Bob joked as he saw the pair approach the judge again.

Suddenly his mother drew her breath in sharply. " Oh, no ! " she exclaimed, " Oh, no ! Surely not ! Oh, what if she's thrown ! "

The judge's voice was heard again. " Ladies and gentlemen, Miss Brownley is now going to attempt to beat the Australian High Jump Record, which stands at eight foot four."

The Brownleys gasped and the mother whitened. " Oh, she shouldn't do it ! " she cried, " what if she's thrown ! "

" Steady, old lady," her husband put a soothing arm around her. " We must pray that she won't," he said.

Jean cantered Diamond up to the hurdle. Dimly, she was conscious that all eyes were upon her and the mare— was conscious, too, that achievement would bring another fifty pounds towards her secret purpose !

" Come on, Diamond," she urged, her voice surprisingly calm, and the mare responded eagerly as she cleared the rail. Higher and higher were the jumps, and Diamond was putting all her strength into it now. Jean could hear her heavy breathing as she flew over eight feet, and returned to the run.

The girl marvelled that Diamond was not nervous, for at each jump the crowd roared its appreciation—enough to have frightened any highly-strung horse.

Eight foot three, and the breathing was heavier now. Jean sat light as a feather, and Diamond leapt into the air to clear the record height. Now, one more jump, and the record would be broken.

" Diamond, you must do this. Oh, Father, please help ! " Jean was desperately excited now, and Diamond was thoroughly roused as she approached the rails.

With one tremendous effort, she hurled herself into the air, and soared over eight foot five ! "

" Hurrah ! " The Brownleys, one and all, let out a hearty yell. " I knew she'd do it ! " Mr. Brownley shouted, " Oh, thank God ! "

They rushed out from the crowd, brushing past spectators in their hurry, and were there at the Marshalling Yard when the victor, having been acclaimed by the judge, was ushered out amid a fresh burst of applause.

" Oh, Jeanie ! " Mrs. Brownley greeted her daughter. " How wonderful ! "

The family crowded around the steaming mare, praising her as never before.

" Look ! " Jean cried suddenly, for over their heads she could see reporters and photographers approaching. Lights flashed and cameras clicked, and then a newsreel photographer was shooting the scene—he had already taken shots of the jumping. If Jean had thirsted for honour, she had her full share now.

" Have you anything to say, Miss Brownley ? " he asked. And as he asked, Jean heard that still small voice, reminding her that God had granted her prayer, and that He is glad when His children give Him their thanks.

For a moment the girl hesitated . . . it would not be easy to thank Him in such a practical way, but as her heart overflowed again with gratitude for all that God had done, she said, " Yes. I know that all this is the answer to prayer, and that all the glory belongs to God."

The reporters wrote busily in the little silence that followed. Some of the crowd murmured something, and Jean realized that her speech had been recorded, and would be seen and heard in newspapers and newsreels everywhere. " O Father," she prayed quickly, " please use it for the glory of Thy Name."

Diamond was really tired after her ordeal, and rested all that morning, but after dinner the final Grand Parade was held, and she appeared, her neck covered with ribbons, in the arena once more.

The Show rose to a grand ending, and one and all were fully satisfied.

That evening, as the Brownleys were relaxing in the lounge of the boarding-house, Jean burst into the room, her face aglow, and thrust something into Bob's hand.

" What's this? "   The boy stared at several notes and three shillings.

" Diamond's prize money," Jean grinned delightedly. " A hundred and sixty-three pounds.   And three guineas for my riding the winning horse in the high jump.   That's a hundred and sixty-six pounds, three shillings.   I thought it would help pay for your Uni. course."

Bob's mouth opened.   " But Jean . . ." he began.

" Go on, take it," urged Jean.   " Mum said that we had nearly enough money for your training, and I thought that would help."

In a flash, the explanation was clear to Mrs. Brownley. " So that's why you did it, Jean," she said.

" Yes, Mummy.   You see, riding's my one talent, so I gave it back to God, and He'll use it for His glory."

Bob was overcome.   " Jean ! Oh, Jean ! " he exclaimed, and then words failed him.

" It's from the Lord, Bob," his sister murmured, " not from me."

" I knew Diamond was meant for something," Jean said some time later, " I always said so, didn't I ? "   For Diamond was undoubtedly one means of enabling Bob to train.

The Brownleys were to return to their station as soon as possible, but they had to remain at the Showground for three days to complete official formalities.

It was on Tuesday, while Jean, with Bob and the youngsters, was watching the sales always held after the Show, that the man sitting next to her remarked interestedly, " You're the lass who owns that mare Black Diamond, aren't you? "

" Yes, my name is Jean Brownley," Jean smiled happily.

" She certainly is a wonderful horse.   I saw her beat the record yesterday, and it was a thrill just to watch her."

" You're a lover of horses? " the girl asked pleasantly.

A low chuckle answered her. " Well, I guess I am, rather. The name's Arthur Beanbrooke."

Jean gasped, for that name was a household word with horse-breeders. " The horse expert? Oh, my hat ! " she exclaimed, delighted.

Mr. Beanbrooke grinned. " Yes," he said, " and that's why I'm interested in Black Diamond. What's her pedigree? "

" Well, we don't know, really. We found her with a herd of brumbies, but we knew she came of better stock."

" My word, she's no brumby ! I say, do you mind if I have a look at her? " So together they went to the horse pavilion, where Mr. Beanbrooke made a thorough critical examination of the black mare.

He refused to tell Jean anything until he had tried out her paces, and studied her minutely. At last, he turned to the girl, and with a slow, almost triumphant smile, he said, " Jean, I'm sure Black Diamond is a thoroughbred ! "

" Really? Oh, is she? " Jean's eyes widened with surprise and delight. " Oh, no wonder she's so marvellous ! Then how could she have come to be with the brumbies? "

" She may have been lost, or stolen, or perhaps she ran away. It's a bit of a mystery."

They stabled the mare, and were returning to the sale ring, when Mr. Beanbrooke stopped dead, a light breaking over his face. " Of course ! Why ever didn't I think of it ! "

" What? " Jean was puzzled.

" Jean, let's go back. I have some suspicions."

Wonderingly, Jean followed him back to the pavilion, where they approached Diamond's stall, Mr. Beanbrooke thinking all the time, ' Black filly, with white diamond and socks. Black filly, with white diamond and socks.'

" How long have you had her? " he asked at length.

" We found her last August. She was nearly two years old."

" Ah, yes ! And where? "

" Oh, some miles north of Aruntoora," Jean replied.

" Yes ! "   Mr. Beanbrooke was getting excited.   " This all fits in perfectly.   Where's Mr. Brownley? "

Later that day, Mr. Beanbrooke having consulted a stud book, had a long talk with Mr. Brownley. At last, the two men came up to where Jean was impatiently waiting, and Mr. Brownley said, "Jean, dear, Mr. Beanbrooke has looked up a stud book, and he feels certain that Black Diamond was one of the horses stolen from his station more than two years ago. Her dam, who was the famous Jane Grey, was stolen too, and we think that she must have died, as she was so old, and Diamond escaped and joined the brumbies. That accounts for her being so wild and independent. Her sire was Eldershade II, so no wonder Diamond is so wonderful ! "

Jean tried to take in all this startling news. " Oh," she gasped. " Oh, how lovely ! But, Dad, what's wrong? "

For Mr. Brownley's look was serious. " Jean," he said, as though the words were being whipped out of him, " you know that Diamond will have to be returned, don't you? "

In her excitement, Jean had forgotten this, and the words struck her as a blow. For a moment, she was rendered speechless, and the colour drained from her face ; then with something like a moan, she turned and ran away.

All that evening the Brownleys discussed Black Diamond, and sought in vain some solution to the problem. Bob's noble suggestion was that with the money saved for his training, they could buy Diamond back, but Jean, in all her grief, would not hear of it.

In bed that night, trying to control quiet sobs, she realized that Diamond had now fulfilled the purpose for which she had been sent. She had helped to enable Bob to go to University, and there was no knowing how many lives and, what was more important, souls, would be saved through the boy's ministry. It seemed to Jean that Diamond's task in her life had now been completed, and if she was to go, this was the right time : it all seemed to fit into the plan.

So Jean, with a calm courage that surprised her, gave her horse back to God, Who gives every gift, and from that moment, a deep sense of peace filled her heart. Humbly she thanked her Heavenly Father for giving her the joy of Diamond's companionship for so long, and for using Diamond to fulfil His purpose.

On the day of the Brownleys' departure, Mr. Beanbrooke came into Diamond's stall and found Jean and the mare " talking " to each other with all the ardour of loved ones bidding farewell.

At the sight of them, the hard-headed business man suddenly gave way to a kind-hearted human, passionately in love with all animals.

He thought of the horses in his stables and knew that he did not need Black Diamond . . . knew also that the mare could never be so happy away from the mistress she loved.

A battle raged in his heart ; Diamond was very valuable, especially after breaking the Australian High Jump Record, but still, in all his wealth, he would not miss her. Besides, what right had he to take the horse away from her rightful owner—rightful because of the love between them?

He knew Diamond could never be his, but would always belong to the girl whose love had tamed the mare and bound them closely together with an unbreakable cord.

" Are you . . . going to take her . . . now? " Jean asked slowly, her face averted to hide the sorrow in her eyes.

Mr. Beanbrooke roused, and gave one searching look at horse and girl. " Jean," he said, equally as slow, " you keep her. She is yours. You belong together, because you love each other. She will never be mine, and I don't really need her. So you keep her." He laid an understanding hand on her shoulder. " And I wish you every happiness together."

As before, Jean was rendered utterly speechless. Her mouth opened as she gazed up at the man, and her mind reeled as she tried to readjust herself. She had been steeling herself against Diamond's departure, and almost pinched herself to make sure she was awake.

" Oh-h-h-h-h ! "   With one cry of unutterable joy, she flung her arms around his neck, crying, " Thank you, oh, thank you ! Oh, is it really true? Oh, I know I can't thank you enough ! "

Diamond came over to them, and Jean buried her face in her mane as she hugged her horse. Diamond gave a soft little snort of happiness.

Mr. Beanbrooke smiled contentedly and left the two together.

20

"BOB! Margaret! Frank! Look, there they are!"

Jean jumped up and down in her excitement, on Aruntoora Railway Station late one afternoon nearly eighteen months later, for from a window of the train just steaming in, Bob, Margaret, and Frank were craning their necks and waving gaily.

Bob was returning to the Brownleys' station after his second term at Sydney University, where he was studying medicine, and the youngsters were coming home from the boarding-schools which had reopened after the epidemic.

The train pulled up with a rattle, a screech, and a bump, and the three seized their suitcases and literally hurled themselves out of the train and into their mother's arms. They embraced their father and Jean with fierce ardour, and then they all bundled into the truck, and started for home.

"Gee, Bob! I've missed you!" Jean said as they walked towards the house together. Few had realized what the separation had meant to the inseparables, and now that Bob had come home, it seemed too good to be true.

Of course, Jean had missed the lively youngsters, too, but they were really on a different level from the older children, and the bond between them was therefore of a different nature.

"Yes, Jeanie, I've missed you a heap, too," was the warm response, "and it's awfully good to be home! I say! How's Black Diamond? I'd nearly forgotten all about her," he teased.

"Black Diamond?" Jean's blank face belied the twinkle in her eye. "You mean the old black nag?"

Bob laughed and continued, "I thought you would have ridden her down; you said in your last letter that she hasn't had much exercise lately."

"Oh, she's all right—in fact, she's tophole." Jean dropped her eyes, determined to keep the secret yet.

Around the tea table questions and answers followed each other in rapid succession, for though the scholars had given all the information about the schools in their letters, nothing is so satisfying as hearing it first-hand.

Bob described the Sydney University once more—the great assembly hall, the cloisters and colonnades, the round of lectures and study.

He had quickly made friends with three other Christian boys, joined the Evangelical Union, and had soon settled down happily. At the E. U. he had met a girl a little younger than he, and when he spoke of her, the sensitive ears of his mother and sister caught a hidden depth.

Mrs. Brownley regarded her elder son over the teapot. He certainly was a man now, she thought. She had had reports of his success—he had quickly risen to the top of his year, and constantly maintained that position. The Brownleys had thought he was rather brainy—he had proved that at his boarding-school—but they had never guessed that he would excel as he had done.

At last he seemed to have finished his story, and the youngsters took up the cue, relating some of the many scrapes they had almost unwittingly " got themselves into ". It had always been the same—the youngsters were capable of transforming the dullest term into a history of exciting escapades.

After tea and family prayer, Bob suggested that he and the youngsters should go and see the horses, so in the gathering dusk the three made their way to the horse paddock while Jean helped to wash up.

When they returned, Bob remarked, a little puzzled, " We couldn't find Black Diamond. Where is she, Jean? "

" Black Diamond? " the girl replied in an off-hand, innocent tone, " Oh, she must be somewhere. You missed her, I s'pose. Anyway, it's too dark to look for her now. You'll see her in the morning."

Bob looked at the speaker. What had Jean got up her sleeve now? Her tone had not passed the notice of her observant brother, but he decided to say nothing.

Far into the night the family talked reminiscently about this and that ; how God had answered prayer in enabling Bob to train, how He had helped him right from the start of his course, and many other things, until finally yawns became apparent, and Mrs. Brownley suggested that bed was the best place.

Next morning Jean woke early with a peculiar sense that someone was calling her. Automatically her thoughts turned to Black Diamond, and after her Bible-reading and prayer, she dressed hastily and went outside.

Had Bob been there, he would have known the reason for Diamond's mysterious disappearance, for the mare was in the stable. Jean entered to find Diamond lying on the straw, her neck stretched out.

Suppressing a cry, she went up to her and gently held her head, murmuring encouragingly to the mare.

Bob woke soon after his sister, and went into her bedroom to suggest a walk before breakfast. Finding her bed empty, however, he dressed and went outside to look for her.

" I wonder where she is? " he mused, and then stood still, for through the calm morning air he could hear a voice—Jean's voice—the voice she used for animals, and he hastened towards the stable.

" Oh, Bob ! " Jean looked up from the hay, and relief overspread her face. " Thank goodness you've come ! "

Bob entered, and in a moment took in the scene. Summoning all his knowledge, he bent over Diamond's prostrate figure and gave Jean a few orders. The girl held Diamond's head and noted that the mare had broken out in a sweat.

She could hear Bob's grunts and words of encouragement. " Steady there, girlie. Take it easy now."

At last, after a time of suspense for both Bob and Jean, the boy uttered a low but exultant cry.

Diamond rose slowly to her feet, swaying a little, and started to lick the little black colt that lay panting on the hay.

" Oh, isn't he lovely? " Jean exclaimed delightedly, and ran back to the house to tell the others. Just out of bed, they followed her, seething with excitement.

" Isn't he lovely? " she exclaimed again. The colt scrambled shakily to his feet, as Diamond regarded the company a little anxiously: he was black except for a thin white streak down his nose.

" Oh, he's a gem ! " Mrs. Brownley cried.

" He's yours, Jean," her husband put in, " I promised you Black Diamond's first foal."

" Oh, Dad, he's lovely. Thank you awfully ! What shall I call him? "

The people stood surveying the pair—Black Diamond with her head stretched lovingly over the colt who was rapidly finding his legs.

"He's rather a forward youngster, isn't he?" Bob remarked. "Diamond's colt *would* be pretty intelligent."

Jean stepped forward, and laid one hand on Diamond's neck, and one on the foal's. She looked at them both and sighed a great sigh of contentment.

"I'll call you Black Gem," she murmured to the foal, "and may you shine as brightly as your mother."

THE END